Himes Charles Francis

A Sketch of Dickinson College, Carlisle, Penn'a

Himes Charles Francis

A Sketch of Dickinson College, Carlisle, Penn'a

ISBN/EAN: 9783337056650

Printed in Europe, USA, Canada, Australia, Japan

Cover: Foto ©Andreas Hilbeck / pixelio.de

More available books at **www.hansebooks.com**

John Dickinson

A SKETCH

OF

DICKINSON COLLEGE,

CARLISLE, PENN'A,

INCLUDING THE LIST OF TRUSTEES AND FACULTY FROM
THE FOUNDATION, AND A MORE PARTICULAR
ACCOUNT OF THE

SCIENTIFIC DEPARTMENT,

BY

CHARLES F. HIMES, PH. D.
PROFESSOR OF NATURAL SCIENCE.

ILLUSTRATED BY ENGRAVINGS, AND BY PHOTOGRAPHS EXE-
CUTED IN THE LABORATORY.

" Pietate et doctrina tuta libertas."
COLLEGE SEAL.

HARRISBURG:
LANE S. HART.
1879.

TO THE FRIENDS OF

HIGHER EDUCATION

IN THE

PATRONIZING CONFERENCES OF THE

METHODIST EPISCOPAL CHURCH,

WHOSE FOSTERING CARE

DICKINSON COLLEGE

HAS ENJOYED FOR HALF A CENTURY.

CONTENTS.

ILLUSTRATIONS.

FULL PAGE.

WOOD CUTS IN TEXT.

PREFACE.

HILST America has made history rapidly, it has been careless in its preservation. The celebration of the National Centennial especially directed attention to this fact. Colleges are by no means exceptions to this general statement. Few of them have at command the material for a satisfactory history. Many of the facts concerning the earlier history of Dickinson College have been lost. A few have recently been rescued, together with many of National and State history, from the paper-stock of a rag-man's loft, and there are many scattered documents of equal interest. This little sketch of the College, written under heavy press of other duties, *currente calamo*, is in no sense a complete history, and no regard has been paid, in its preparation, to symmetrical treatment. But fragmentary and incomplete as it is, it is, perhaps, more of a history of the College than has as yet appeared, and will serve, at least, as a nucleus around which to accumulate the material for a more satisfactory account of the College, perhaps by the date of its Centennial—1883. An Alumni Record, containing the prominent facts in the life of each Alumnus would, in that connection, be of the highest interest, and if undertaken in time, with the hearty coöperation of all the friends of the College, might be completed by the date mentioned.

The separate and fuller treatment of the history of the Scientific Department of the College, has its explanation in the suggestion of such a history as a possible auxiliary in carrying out a resolution of the Board of Trustees, authorizing the writer to raise funds for the erection of a new building for scientific purposes. In the course of investigation, in that direction, facts of more general interest manifested themselves, and the plan was expanded so as to incorporate many of them.

As descriptions, with statements of dimensions, convey but feeble impressions in regard to the character, size, and surroundings of buildings, pictorial representation of these essential features of a college has been attempted by the aid of photography. The photographs, printed as they have been, in the laboratory, by amateurs, at odd intervals, in large numbers, are not given as specimens of that art, but it is hoped that they may serve, at least, as satisfactory notes to the alumni and friends of the College. The plate of the case of apparatus is given on account of the scientific interest attached to the historic pieces it includes.

By the favor of Harper & Brothers, it has been possible to present the excellent portrait of Doctor Durbin.

C. F. H.

Dickinson College, *June*, 1879.

Chapter I.

FOUNDATION OF THE COLLEGE.

State of the Country—Origin of Dickinson College—
Motives of Founders—Name—Collegiate Education
in the Country—Carlisle.

HE treaty of 1783, which closed the Revolutionary struggle with the acknowledgment of the Independence of the Colonies, ends so happily the narrative of tedious and wasting campaigns, and of earnest and anxious deliberations full of discouragements of every character, that the actual condition of the new nation is apt to be lost sight of, especially after the event has been so greatly magnified, in its consequences, by the lapse of a century. Besides the grateful relief from the immediate burdens and anxieties incident to a state of war, there was little else in the state of affairs that was hopeful or inspiring. The public resources had been taxed to the utmost, and the prevalence of wide-spread distrust, with the universal depression, prevented the inception of recuperative enterprises. Without public credit, without commerce, with industries paralyzed, with an irredeemable paper currency, unstable and wanting in uniformity at best, depreciated to worthlessness, and with society honey-combed by all the demoralizing influences that follow in the wake of war, with a Federal Government that had owed all its consistency to the presence of a common danger, rapidly resolving itself into its original, rather discordant, elements, with State Governments, for the most part creatures of revolution,

threatened by new revolution, the situation was well calculated
to render capital timid, repress enterprise, and cause the most
profound anxiety to the most thoughtful patriots of that day.
A government at once the strongest, and freest, and the most
enlightened that the world had known, had been exchanged for
a form of government ill-defined, untried, and revolutionary,
and resting upon the entirely new basis of purely popular will.
Whilst independence seemed secure, personal rights and liberties could only be rendered secure from anarchy on the one
hand, or despotism on the other hand, by the adjustment
into a harmonious whole of the multitudinous conflicting, almost
irreconcilable interests that clashed on every side. To declare
independence required courage, to carry on the war required
sacrifices, which pride with patriotism dictated, but to bring
political order and stability out of the apparent chaos, to in-
spire confidence in the people in themselves and their surroundings, and stimulate them to new undertakings required in the
leaders a reserve force of statesmanship and of unselfish patriotism, which had not been drawn upon during the trying times
of the revolution. To these demands they measured up so
fully, that their after work of the consolidation of a nation out
of such elements, must remain the marvel of that period.

During the war educational interests had been largely neglected. Schools of lower grade, as well as colleges, had sus-
pended. Judged by the ordinary and usual standards, the times
would have been considered very inauspicious for the inauguration of large educational enterprises. The suggestion to found
a college in a sparsely settled region one hundred miles further
west of the Atlantic than any other, to meet future rather than
present necessities, would have been considered rather inop-
portune. And yet leading men coöperated in urging through
the Legislature of Pennsylvania a charter for such an institution—the second in the State—and the first meeting of the

Board of Trustees of Dickinson College was held at the house
of Governor Dickinson, in Philadelphia, on the 15th of September, 1783, one week after the charter had been secured, and
organized by electing him as its president. The project was
not altogether a new one. The establishment of a college at
some point west of the Susquehanna had been agitated before
the Revolution, by some prominent gentlemen. Among the
obstacles encountered was the refusal of the Colonial Legislature to grant the necessary charter, a cause of failure that can
hardly be deemed sufficient, or even be comprehended at this
time, when any academy can have conferred upon it all the
rights, privileges, and immunities of a university for the asking.
At the first announcement of the close of the war, however,
the interest of patriotic and liberal-hearted citizens of the State
centered anew in this object, as one of the most effective measures for the preservation and proper fruition of the liberties just
achieved. It had also acquired a new importance, since it seemed
but proper that the youth of now independent America should
be educated at home, rather than in the schools of England, as
had been very customary before the war. The motives that
inspired the founders of the college, as well as the character
of the assurances that were required by the legislators of that
day, before granting such privileges, are set forth so fully, and
with such evident care, in the preamble and enacting clause of
the charter, that its insertion here seems but just, as well as
proper :

SECTION I. *Whereas*, The happiness and prosperity of every
community, (under the direction and government of Divine
Providence,) depends much on the right education of the youth,
who must succeed the aged in the important offices of society,
and the most exalted nations have acquired their pre-eminence
by the virtuous principles and liberal knowledge instilled into
the minds of the rising generation ;

SECTION II. *And whereas,* After a long and bloody contest with a great and powerful kingdom, it has pleased Almighty God to restore to the United States of America the blessings of a general peace, whereby the good people of this State, relieved from the burthens of war, are placed in a condition to attend to useful arts, sciences, and literature, and it is the evident duty and interest of all ranks of people to promote and encourage, as much as in them lies, every attempt to disseminate and promote the growth of useful knowledge;

SECTION III. *And whereas,* By the petition of a large number of persons of established reputation for patriotism, integrity, ability, and humanity, presented to this House, it appears that the institution of a College at the Borough of Carlisle, in the County of Cumberland, for the instruction of youth in the learned languages, and other branches of literature, is likely to promote the real welfare of this State, and especially of the western parts thereof;

SECTION IV. *And whereas,* This House is informed, as well by the said petition as by other authentic documents, that a large sum of money, sufficient to begin and carry on the design, for some considerable time, is already subscribed by the generous liberality of divers persons, who are desirous to promote so useful an institution, and there is no doubt but that further donations will be voluntarily made, so as to carry it into perfect execution: And this House, cheerfully concurring in so laudable a work;

SECTION V. *Be it therefore enacted, and it is hereby enacted by the Representatives of the Freemen of the Commonwealth of Pennsylvania, in General Assembly met, and by the authority of the same,* That there be erected, and hereby is erected and established, in the Borough of Carlisle, in the County of Cumberland, in this State, a College, for the education of youth in the learned and foreign languages, the useful arts, sciences, and literature, the style, name, and title of which said College, and the Constitution thereof, shall be and are hereby declared to be as is hereafter mentioned and defined ; that is to say,

1. In memory of the great and important services rendered to his country by his Excellency John Dickinson, Esquire, President of the Supreme Executive Council, and in commemoration of his very liberal donation to the Institution, the said College shall be forever hereafter called and known by the name of " Dickinson College."

The provisions for collegiate education in the country, at this time, consisted in one college in each of the then New England States, one in New York—Columbia, formerly King's ; two in New Jersey—Rutger's, formerly Queen's, and the College of New Jersey, at Princeton ; two in Virginia, including William and Mary, perhaps the most liberally endowed college on the Continent, and after Harvard, the oldest. Pennsylvania had also one representative of institutions of this grade, in the University of Pennsylvania, established in 1755. The colleges, however, were all small in endowment and in number of students, and feeble in the numerical strength of their faculties. Thus, Columbia College had but two professors and twenty-four students, and the College of New Jersey was considered flourishing with two professors, in addition to the Provost, and sixty students. The sentiment of the country, however, may be said to have been favorable to institutions of the higher grade. The leading Colonies, even in their early feebleness and poverty, had made sacrifices to establish them, and had aided and encouraged them in every way. Whilst the education of the ministry was generally a prominent thought in the minds of the originators of them, their graduates were soon found in prominent positions in the State, and had much to do in molding its character. During the war the colleges, as a rule, with but few exceptions, were unequivocally on the side of the Government. Harvard alone, contributed seven graduates to the Congress that declared independence, and nearly half of the signers of that immortal document were graduates of American or European colleges, and of the remainder, the majority, with some very notable exceptions, had received a training almost equivalent to that of the college. The influence of the educated man was due to the more general diffusion of intelligence in the Colonies, at that time, than in the leading countries of the world, and the forcible, skillfully written essays, multiplied by the press, were potent in forming and controling public sentiment.

The selection of Carlisle as the new seat of learning was a very natural one. Beautifully situated in the midst of the fertile and healthy Cumberland Valley, it was surrounded by an intelligent and enterprising population, calculated to profit by and encourage an institution of the kind. It had been the seat of justice of the county since 1751, although it had, in 1753, but five houses. At the foundation of the College it had, probably, less than fifteen hundred inhabitants, with scarcely a stage coach connection with the outer world. During the war, in its connection with the county, it had been favorably introduced to the leading statesmen of the country. It had nobly borne its share in field, and was very prominent in advocating all the advanced measures of the colonies, and first urged separation from the mother country upon the tardy Assembly of Pennsylvania. Its companies formed a part of the first rifle regiment, under Colonel Thompson, of Cumberland county, which embraced the first companies from south of the Hudson to arrive in Massachusetts after the battle of Bunker Hill, and that command became, in January, 1776, "the first regiment of the army of the United Colonies, under General George Washington." Among the contributions of the county to the revolutionary army were Magaw, Armstrong, Irvine, the five Butler brothers, and others, whilst, during the dark days of the winter at Valley Forge, Ephraim Blaine, grandfather of Senator Blaine, as Commissary General, by the use of his private fortune and credit, made it possible for Washington to hold together his suffering and disintegrating army. As the town was remote from the seat of war, it was made a place of rendezvous for recruits and of confinement for prisoners. During his first captivity Major André was on parole in the town, and the Hessians captured at Trenton were employed in the erection of the barracks in the northeastern limits of the borough. These have remained a United States military post to the present time. They will garrison two thousand men, and have been the home at different times of some of the leading officers on both sides during the late war. On the night of July 1, 1863, they were burned by order of General Fitz Hugh Lee, but have since been reconstructed so accurately upon the same plan, that the student of *ante bellum* times would scarcely suspect that they had experienced the rough usages of war.

CHAPTER II.

THE FOUNDERS.

BOARD OF TRUSTEES—GOVERNOR DICKINSON AND DR. BENJ. RUSH—DICKINSON'S DONATION—SKETCH OF DICKINSON.

HE first Board of Trustees under the act of incorporation, composed of forty members, embraced many men of the highest prominence in the State. More than one third of the number, according to that act, consisted of clergymen. The reason for the presence of so many of the latter, and their general relation to the College, as well as the position of the clergy at that time with reference to higher education, can be best comprehended by an inspection of the following section in the original charter: "As it has been found by experience that those persons separated from the busy scenes of life, that they may with more attention study the grounds of the Christian religion and minister it to the people, are in general zealous promotors of the education of youth, and cheerfully give up their time and attention to objects of this kind; therefore, whenever a vacancy shall happen, by want of qualification, resignation, or decease of any clergyman hereby appointed a trustee, such vacancy shall be filled by the choice of another clergyman of any Christian denomination, and so *toties quoties* such vacancy shall happen, whereby the number of clergymen hereby appointed shall never be lessened." This clause was modified by the Legislature, in 1826, so as to

read : "That not more than one third of the trustees shall, at any one time, be clergymen."

From the number of the incorporators, there is good reason to select Governor Dickinson and Dr. Benjamin Rush, one of the signers of the Declaration of Independence, as those to whom, more than all the others, the college owed its origin and its growth. The name of the one, as has been stated, was given to it by the Legislature, on account of his great and important services to his country, and in commemoration of his very liberal donation. The other, by his unwearied, enthusiastic personal efforts, extending over more than a quarter of a century, perhaps contributed more largely to the permanent establishment of the institution. There is scarcely a subject connected with the organization and successful conduct of a college that has not been touched upon in the fragments that remain of his voluminous correspondence in regard to it. At one time deeply concerned about the selection of a principal or of an instructor, at another time about the healthfulness of the location, about suitable provisions for instruction in the way of philosophical apparatus, books, &c., and at all times about the collection of funds, and their most judicious investment or expenditure, he was not wanting in generous contributions of money, as well as time. At times he appears to have been almost the life as well as the inspiration of the corporation. When others became disheartened, his faith in the ultimate success of the enterprise seemed unshaken, and his tone was as cheerful and enthusiastic as in the earlier days. As late as 1808, twenty-five years after the founding of the College, he closes a long letter in regard to some business connected with it, as follows: "My dear old friend, in writing you upon the subject of our College, I feel *now* all the ardor I felt at its establishment." The italics are his.

It would be difficult to find two individuals more widely diverse in many leading traits of character and in opinions than the two named as leading spirits in this enterprise, in regard to which they were singularly in accord. Both were highly educated, polished gentlemen : both had had unusual prominence in public life during a time calculated to display more fully than usual a man's whole character, and though the patriotism of neither could be called in question, they had differed, radically, upon the leading question of that day. No more satisfactory reason for attaching the name of Dickinson to the College could be desired, than that just given from the charter. His position as a trusted political leader was calculated to give character to the young institution, whilst the more substantial aid of his liberal donation, perhaps, alone rendered its inauguration possible. The exact nature and extent of the donation alluded to, is not known. A "plantation" of two hundred acres on Marsh creek, York county, now Adams county, at least formed a part of it. A valuable collection of books from his library, which was one of the most valuable in the country, accompanied it. He subsequently added a "plantation" of five hundred acres in Cumberland county, with the condition of an annuity to Doctor Nisbet. The term "plantation" characterized improved lands, which were readily saleable, and therefore equivalent to cash. With thousands of acres of wild lands in its possession, donated by different individuals, the Board of Trustees at an early day disposed of the plantation first alluded to for £200. There were doubtless other similar minor evidences of his interest in the College. After a friendly visit of Doctor Nisbet to him at his home in Wilmington, Delaware, in 1792, he notified him on his return to Carlisle, that $500 had been deposited in one of the Philadelphia banks subject to his order, to defray the expense of future visits which he had solicited. But taking all his donations together, although the sum may have been all that it was described to be for that day, it would scarcely be considered large at this time. Large donations from individuals to higher institutions of learning were hardly known a century ago, not only because accumulated private fortunes were not as great then, but, also, because there did not appear to be the same necessity for them when such institutions were more especially regarded as entitled to the fostering care of the State, and were aided by it as their necessities seemed to require. It was expected that Dickinson would receive such recognition from the State, an expectation that was not disappointed. A true estimate of Governor Dickinson's donation can, perhaps, best be made by a comparison, as with that of Yale, that gave his name to a college already established, which did not exceed £500 in "goods" and books.

Although the name and prominence of an individual may contribute much to the early character and success of an institution, the direct potency of personal association ceases with the lapse of a generation or two, the name becomes a secondary matter and presents but a feeble claim to public patronage or confidence. And yet the somewhat sentimental attachment that imparts an importance to even the most trifling incidents connected with a literary Alma Mater, must continue to invest the name and character of its most prominent patron with some interest for the sons of old Dickinson, and demand for him more than simply a brief mention in connection with any sketch of the College.

The name of John Dickinson is encountered very frequently in turning the pages of American history, from the earliest period of colonial restiveness under the unwarranted interference of the goverment of the mother country up to the final act, and subsequent hostilities, that completely severed their political connection. But, whilst the task of the historian has been comparatively easy and pleasant in dealing with the characters of the leading patriots of that period who advocated independence, it has often been a matter of exceed-

2

ing delicacy to assign their proper influence, and the true motives to those who seem to stand out as obstacles to the popular current.   With regard to the former the errors of critical
judgment are necessarily confined to what, by comparison,
might be termed the minor details of character, whilst with
the latter all the leading traits of unselfish patriotism, of
courage, of political sagacity, and honor are more or less involved.   Thus there are acts in the public life of Dickinson
which the kindly disposed may see only as the subordinate
features of a pure, beautiful, and consistently patriotic character, but which others may keep in such undue and continual
prominence as to produce a distorted impression, and do great
injustice to a man who, in his way, performed a part perhaps
as effective in realizing the fondest wishes of the most ardent
patriots of that day as any other who figured in the history of
those times, and a part demanding as great a measure of courage, especially of moral courage, as many acts that seem
bolder.   At the same time, no greater tribute to his ability as a
popular leader can be made than that involved in the great
influence attributed to him by those who would most detract
from his character.   A brief consideration of the most salient
points of his history, after the lapse of a century, it is believed,
will exhibit him as a far-sighted statesman, as well as a thorough American in all his sympathies and conduct.

A native of Maryland, born in 1732, of Quaker parentage,
he became identified in his interests and political history with
the States of Pennsylvania and Delaware, by the removal of
his father, a few years after his birth, to Kent county, in the
latter State, where he was Presiding Judge, and proprietor of
a large landed estate.   Thus, although a Quaker by descent,
he neither adhered rigidly to their peculiar form of speech, nor
to their practices in regard to military service, but in the correspondence of his later years with his intimate friends this

Quaker element in his character crops out in his language, and is a factor never to be lost sight of in interpreting his public as well as private life. Little is known in regard to his early education, except that Chancellor Killen, when a young man, was his tutor. The loss, by death, of two of his brothers in England, whither they had been sent, as was common at that time, to be educated, undoubtedly influenced the father in the education of this son ; but the wonderful classical attainments manifested in all his literary productions leave no doubt as to the thoroughness of his instruction. The opinion expressed by Jefferson, that he was " one of the most accomplished scholars that the country has produced," was but the prevalent opinion of his eminent political associates. After pursuing the study of law in Philadelphia, he spent three years in the Temple in London, and subsequently practiced his profession in Philadelphia. As a lawyer he was profoundly read and of clear judgment, and enjoyed a recognized prominence in the Colonies. He began his political career as one of the members of the Assembly of Pennsylvania from the county of Philadelphia, in 1764, where he opposed a petition for a change of the government of the Province from Proprietary to Royal, in a very effective speech. Although this was three months before the passage of the Stamp Act, he suggested forcibly the designs of the British Ministry upon the liberties of the Colonies, and urged that " with unremitting vigilance, with undaunted virtue, should a free people watch against the encroachments of power and remove every pretext for its extension."

In 1765, as one of the three deputies from Pennsylvania to the first Colonial Congress in New York, he drafted the principal resolutions passed by that body. His eloquent pen was frequently effectually employed in discussing the great questions that were thrusting themselves into prominence in the

Colonies, and he unquestionably holds the position as the leading essayist upon those questions.   The letters over the signature of "A Farmer," published in 1767, were, perhaps, most
widely known, as well as the most effective.   They were re-
published by Franklin, in England, and were also translated
into French, so that that *nom de plume* became his title where-
ever the American question was discussed.   Clear, simple, eloquent, and forcible in style, abounding in illustrations, founded
upon an examination of all the statutes since the settlement of
the Colonies, they set forth, exhaustively, their rights and
grievances, and in such a way as to impress the Colonists that
a "most dangerous innovation" upon their liberties was about
to be attempted by the British ministry; and whilst his recommendation was "immediately, vigorously, and unanimously to
exert themselves in the most firm, but the most peaceable manner, for obtaining relief," he added, "if an inveterate resolution is formed to annihilate the liberties of the governed, English history affords examples of resistance by force."   As Bancroft says: "The Farmer's letters carried conviction through
the Thirteen Colonies."   They accomplished much in uniting
the Colonies in sympathy and action.   Their effect may be
very properly estimated in connection with the essay entitled
"Common Sense," of a later date, to which exaggerated
prominence is so frequently given.   The former preceded public sentiment, and, in a great measure, formed it; they were a
calm, dispassionate appeal to reason, to love of liberty, and
patriotism; the latter was not only based on public opinion
already formed, but owed its popularity, in great degree, to
its consonance with excited public feeling, inflamed and ready
for war.   But above all, behind the former was a character acknowledged to be pure, honest, irreproachable, and unpur-
chasable, very apparently permeated with love of country and
humanity, and withal of known conservatism; a character to

which the Continental Congress often deferred, even when he stood almost alone in his views and wishes in regard to measures of greatest public moment. The author of the other was a political and social adventurer, a low, intemperate and untruthful fellow, a venÿal writer, without principle, a product of the worst influences of French society. He was termed by John Adams, "a disastrous meteor," and he, perhaps, best estimated his pamphlet as having had little effect in converting those to the cause of independence, who would not have followed Congress with zeal, whilst it repelled some of the most influential from the cause.*

Nowhere was the appreciation of the Farmer's opportune help more sincere than at Boston. A letter of thanks reported to an adjourned town meeting by a committee, which included Samuel Adams, John Hancock, and Doctor Warren, unanimously adopted, and ordered to be published, set forth the obligations of America to him "for a most seasonable, sensible, loyal, and vigorous vindication of her invaded rights and liberties." The College of New Jersey also added its testimonial in 1769, according to a letter of Madison, then a student there, to his father, by conferring the then unusual honor of LL. D. upon "John Dickinson, the Farmer." As events rapidly developed, his position as an acknowledged political leader in Pennsylvania gave him still more decided prominence in Colonial affairs. It required no ordinary ability to occupy such a position in Pennsylvania, on account of the numerous, conflicting, irreconcilable political factors. Whilst he seems at times to check a popular tendency toward a rupture with Great Britain, and consequent independence, a closer study of the situation shows that he was in advance of the control-

---

*Life and Works of John Adams, Boston, 1851. Vol. ii, p. 153; p. 507; Vol. iii, p. 421; Vol. x, p. 380.

ling elements of the State in this respect, and comprehended
fully the character, influence, and numbers of those who "cherished a passionate desire for reconciliation with the mother
country." The difficulties and influence of his surroundings
are at times hardly appreciated, and even Bancroft, in his ad-
miration for and comprehension of the more rugged virtues of
the Adamses, frequently imparts a tinge of unmeant unkind-
ness and severity to his criticisms of the course of Dickinson.
Thus whilst he speaks of him as having been taught from his
infancy to love humanity and liberty, of his claims to public
respect as indisputable, of the honor showed for his spotless
morals, of his eloquence and services in the Colonial Legislature, and of the writings that had endeared him to America as
a sincere friend of liberty, he speaks of his maturing a "scheme
in the solitude of his retreat" to control the meeting at Philadelphia after the receipt of the Boston port bill, and that he
embodied "with calculating reserve," in a letter to Boston, the
system which for the coming year was to form the policy of
America, a general Congress, and a petition to the King. The
course of Dickinson at this meeting was deliberately fixed upon,
upon consultation with, and with the hearty approval of, Charles
Thompson, Secretary of Congress, and styled for his radical
patriotism, the Sam Adams of Philadelphia. The letter, although it did embody the policy of Dickinson, and was long
attributed to him, proves to have been written by another, and
after all, although it was received with impatience in Boston,
was indorsed by Samuel Adams, who confessed himself "fully
of the Farmer's sentiments; violence and submission would at
this time be equally fatal." The Governor of Pennsylvania
having declined to convene the Assembly, the Committee of
Correspondence of Philadelphia, of which Dickinson was a
member, called a meeting of a Provincial Committee. Among
the delegates from the city and county of Philadelphia, was

Dickinson. Without arrogating any authority, this convention passed resolutions highly loyal, but equally determined for the rights of America, and recommending the appointment, by the Assembly, of delegates to a Continental Congress, and it also appointed a committee on instructions to the delegates that might be chosen, as well as to the Assembly, to define the wishes and policy of the people. In all these measures Dickinson heartily concurred, and the instructions were written by him in his usual style, and accompanied by a lengthy argument. As a result, the Assembly, which was then under the control of Galloway, appointed delegates in order to prevent the selection of them by the Provincial Convention, in case it refused to unite.

The statement of Bancroft, that Dickinson's "elaborate argument, with its 'chilling erudition,' allayed the impassioned enthusiasm of patriotism to such an extent that he was passed by for Galloway, whose loyalty to England was not suspected," hardly fully explains the case. By the intrigue of Galloway, Dickinson, together with the other gentlemen recommended by the convention, was excluded from the number of candidates by a resolution of the Assembly to confine the selection to members of their own body. The absence of Dickinson from the delegation was so marked, that at the ensuing election, in October, he was with practical unanimity elected to the Assembly, and that new body, on the day of its organization, added him to the delegation of the State in the Continental Congress. Here he was at once added to the Committee on the Address to the King, and drafted the paper which, with but little amendment, was adopted by the Congress. "It was a paper penned with extraordinary force and animation, and frequently rising to a high strain of eloquence," and was one of the papers which elicited the celebrated encomium of Chatham upon the Continental Congress. Its authorship was attributed to Adams,

Henry, and Lee, and even at a comparatively recent date, was ascribed by an eminent individual, in an historical address, to John Adams; but there is no longer any question upon this point. He also wrote the "masterly address" to "The Inhabitants of Quebec," a matter of considerable delicacy, in view of the recent acquisition from France.

At this time he resided at his fine country seat of Fair Hill, then one of the suburbs, now a densely populated portion of the city of Philadelphia, surrounded by all the comforts and advantages of wealth, and high social and professional position. His marriage with Miss Mary Norris, the daughter of the Speaker of the Pennsylvania Assembly, had had no tendency to repress his literary or political activity. His mode of life is frequently indicated by John Adams, in his diary. In noting his first meeting with him, he states: "The Farmer of Pennsylvania came in his coach with four beautiful horses to see us." His residence he afterward characterized as "very fine, with its beautiful prospect of the city, the river, the country, fine gardens, and very grand library." The latter was largely the accumulation of his wife's father, and the book-plate of Isaac Norris is found in many of the volumes that formed a part of his donation to the library of the College. With the magnificent hospitality of the Philadelphia of that day, in common with the other leading patriots, he welcomed the delegates from the sister colonies, and earnestly and anxiously discussed the crisis in public affairs. The mansion of Fair Hill was subsequently destroyed by the British, after the battle of Germantown, as the property of the Rebel Dickinson.

After the adjournment of Congress he attended the Assembly and secured the approval of the proceedings of Congress, in spite of the opposition of Galloway. He was a member of the next Congress, as well as of the Provincial Convention ; and upon the receipt of the exciting news from Lexington, he accepted the command of one of the volunteer regiments raised in Philadelphia.

The Congress that met in May, 1875, proceeded cautiously. After many days of anxious discussion, largely in deference to Dickinson's opinions, in spite of the earnest protest of John Adams, it agreed to again petition the King, and the document was prepared by Dickinson, with the only result of causing him to be included by the King, in his proclamation, as a dangerous and designing man. But, besides the petition to the King, which looked toward reconciliation, there were continued preparations for defense by force, and "a declaration of the causes and necessity for taking up arms," was ordered by Congress, and also prepared by Dickinson. Although it sought to quiet the fears of those who were unfavorable to independence, by asserting that "necessity had not driven them into that desperate measure," it also declared, "we cannot endure the infamy and guilt of resigning succeeding generations to that wretchedness which inevitably awaits them, if we basely entail hereditary bondage upon them. We most solemnly and before God DECLARE that, exerting the utmost energy of those powers which our beneficent Creator hath graciously bestowed upon us, the arms we have been compelled by our enemies to assume, we will, in defiance of every hazard, with unabating firmness and perseverance, employ for the preservation of our liberties, being with one mind resolved to die freemen rather than live slaves." According to Bancroft, this declaration was read, on the 15th of July, by the President of Harvard College, to the army of Washington, at Cambridge, and on the 18th it was read at Prospect Hill, amid such shouts that the British on Bunker Hill put themselves in array for battle. It is proper to add that a portion of it is ascribed, by the same eminent authority, to Jefferson, and without mentioning Dickinson's name in connection with it at all, although it appears in full, in the writings of the latter, published in 1801. During this time he was also a member of the Committee of Safety of Pennsylvania, the moving patriot organization of the State, as well as a member of the Assembly. At all times his opinions carried great weight. In Congress, he was also prominent on the Committee on Correspondence with Foreign States, and as a member of that on Confederation, he drew up the plan of confederation reported to Congress, and entered heartily into all military preparations for the defense of the rights of the Colonies.

Although in commenting on the Farmer's Letters, Bancroft remarks that he came forth before the Continent as the champion of American rights, he at the same time none too strongly stated the other side of his character, as an "enthusiast in his love for England," "who accepted the undefined relations of the Parliament to the Colonies as a perpetual compromise." In this he was sustained by the whole country. In the language of the Boston letter of thanks to him, it was by "leaning on the pillars of the British Constitution" that he had "instructed America in the best means to obtain redress." Although the second petition to the King was regarded with impatience by many, it was in accordance with the judgment and ardent wishes of many eminent patriots, and was most certainly consistent with every utterance of Dickinson's, from his entrance into political life. Upon its rejection by the King, the question of independence assumed at once great prominence, and Dickinson became the ablest opponent of an immediate declaration, as John Adams may be regarded as the ablest advocate of that measure. The patriotism, as well as the ability, of neither could be called in question. They were the products and representatives of essentially different political, social, and religious conditions. The impulse for independence came from New England. Those colonies, with

Royal governors, were in frequent conflict with the Crown, their interests clashed continually with Royal prerogative, they became familiarized with the language of opposition and rebellion, and they were the first to feel the oppression and realize the designs of the British Ministry. Pennsylvania, on the other hand, under its proprietary form of government, with many special privileges, in its disputes with the Proprietaries was accustomed to look to the King for relief. Again, Adams was of a people that had always regarded war as a means to accomplish the divine purposes; their acquisitions from the natives were by war, whilst Dickinson was surrounded by influences adverse to war as an agent of good, and the peaceful conquests of his State were regarded by many as the proudest incidents of its history. Add to these influences the conservatism natural to wealth, high social position, and literary tastes, and it seems natural that the Pennsylvania leader should differ on many points from the New Englander. Both were deeply thoughtful, as well as earnest and sincere. Adams no less than Dickinson realized the momentous character of the measure advocated. The petitions to the King were not mere skirmishes for diplomatic position on the part of Dickinson, in a conflict regarded as inevitable. They were sincere in every expression of loyalty, and were written with the earnest hope that they might accomplish their purpose, and that "England might be induced to return to her old good humor, her old good nature." At the same time he was jealous of every right as a British subject under the British constitution, and willing to defend them by force, if necessary. Neither was his view of the destiny of America more contracted or more wanting in range than that of the other. He did not look upon the Continent as an appendage to the British State, but as an integral part of a grand British Empire. An American was to him not simply a reproduced Briton.

"Here," he wrote, as quoted from the first number of "The
Progress," lately published, "individuals of all nations are
melted into a new race of men, whose labors and posterity
will one day cause great changes in the world. Americans are
the Western pilgrims who are carrying along with them that
great mass of arts, sciences, vigor, and industry which began
long since in the East. They will finish the great circle."
Whilst it seems natural that Adams, coming from suffering New
England, with his conclusions as clearly reached in regard to
the ultimate issue as the q. e. d. of a mathematical demonstra-
tion, should have been impatient of any measure or any man
that delayed the inevitable, it was equally natural for Dickinson to court delay as long as any hope of reconciliation could
be entertained. And yet there was no reason why their common, earnest, and unselfish interest in the welfare of what they
regarded as their common country should not have made these
leaders fast friends, in spite of their decided differences on
many points. They met first during the Congress of 1774.
Adams, to use his own words, had found Dickinson a very
modest man and very ingenious, as well as agreeable, with an
excellent heart and the cause of his country near it; he had
spent delightful time with him, had had sweet communion in
which Dickinson gave his thoughts and correspondence very
freely. In the foreign policy of the Colonies, they were fully
in accord. It was during the debate upon the second petition
to the King that an accidental capture of letters written by
Adams, and their publication by the British, led to a lifelong
estrangement, which no one regretted more than Adams. The
fact of the letter, as given by Bancroft, without an intimation
of the regret of Adams for it, hardly does justice to that statesman. He explains in his diary, that he wrote the letter hastily
on account of the importunity of a friend, and at a time when
he was provoked at what he considered a magisterial lecture

from Mr. Dickinson, and smarting even more over his defeat by him in Congress. It the correspondence of his later years, he admits the important part the petitions to the King played, as overlooked by him at the time, and speaks of the reputation of these compositions as a splendid distinction. Considered in all its bearings the statement that Dickinson was the leading opponent of the declaration, impeaches neither his courage, his patriotism, nor his statesmanship. He regarded it as premature. He recognized a great want of unanimity among the colonists, and an earnest faithful body of able friends of America in England. In his view, many measures should have preceded so decisive a step. As he read history, he found cause for fear in the diverse interests and characters, and the jealousies of the several Colonies, and that without an umpire such as they had had in England, they might become a prey to foreign domination. He desired that the most threatening of inter-colonial questions should be settled, and a firm form of confederation established, so that the weight of a united country could be thrown into the contest. He also thought that more favorable terms could be secured from foreign governments before than after a declaration, and was opposed to any measure that looked like sacrificing independence of foreign governments for independence of England. In addition, as a Pennsylvania politician, he understood the great bitterness as well as diversity of feeling existing in that Colony. He felt that he had the confidence of all parties. He had been re-elected after his advocacy of the second petition practically without opposition, in spite of the censures of New England men. Patriots, loyalists, quakers, and the proprietary party had all voted for him. He knew, as Doctor Rush has stated it, that John Adams, after the intercepted letter reflecting on him had been published, had " walked the streets of Philadelphia alone an object of nearly universal scorn and detestation." The instructions of the Assembly that appointed him, were explicit against a declaration of independence. The majority of the Pennsylvania delegation were opposed to it. The Convention called to supersede the regular government of Pennsylvania he regarded as unnecessary and consequently usurpation. The Constitution it adopted on Tom Paine's model was impracticable, and kept the State in a condition bordering on anarchy during the whole war, and for years afterward. However necessary revolutionary measures may have been in other States with royal Governors, the government of Pennsylvania was in the hands of the people, and its patriot leaders felt that they were bringing the people with them to the point, at which the State, through its regularly constituted government, would throw its whole and great weight into the contest. It seemed worth a few months time to accomplish this. It is natural, too, that the interference and dictation should not have been kindly received on the part of the recognized leaders of the State. This view of Dickinson's motives and policy is in accordance with the account of Charles Thompson, the Secretary, who expressed the opinion that "had the whigs in the Assembly been left to pursue their own measures, there is every reason to believe they would have effected their purpose, prevented that disunion which has unhappily taken place, and brought the whole province as one man, with all its force and weight of government, into the common cause."

In the final debate upon independence, when, as Bancroft remarks, he would have held it guilt to suppress his opinions, the ruling motives of his whole public life were condensed in his prefatory remark—"I value the love of my country as I ought, but I value my country more; and I desire this illustrious assembly to witness the integrity if not the policy of my conduct." In considering the effects upon foreign nations of the declaration, he regarded them as immense, and remarked that they "may vibrate around the globe." His position of hesitation is expressed and explained in closing remarks: "Upon the whole, when things shall be thus deliberately rendered firm at home, and favorable abroad, then let America, 'Attollens humeris famam et fata nepotum,' advance with majestic steps, and assume her station among the sovereigns of the world."

This opposition of Dickinson to the Declaration is regarded by Hildreth as "an example of moral courage, of which there are few instances in our history."

The vote of Pennsylvania was then cast against the preliminary resolution for independence by a vote of four to three, and on the final vote, on the following day, Dickinson and Morris, though present in the hall, were not formally present on roll-call, and by thus refusing to vote, permitted the three delegates in favor of independence to out vote the other two, and make the vote on the declaration, by colonies, unanimous. But his whole course is relieved from any suspicion of want of personal courage, or of patriotism, or of disposition to share the fortunes of his colleagues, for he immediately accompanied his regiment to the field, at the flying-camp organized in New Jersey, an act identifying him as clearly with the patriot cause as the most legible signature to the declaration. It is stated as a curious fact, that this, the ablest opponent of independence in Congress, "was the only member of that body, who immediately took up arms to face the enemy." The action is the more marked by its contrast with that of other prominent Pennsylvanians, among them Galloway, his old opponent, and Chief Justice Allen, who soon found their way within the British lines as loyal subjects.

After a short retirement from office, he was again found in the Congress of the nation as a delegate from Delaware. In 1779 he wrote the address to the several States ordered by Congress. In 1782, after one of the most bitter political contests, he was triumphantly elected Executive of Pennsylvania,

although occupying at the time a similar position in Delaware.
The two States were so intimately connected that citizens of one
were eligible to offices in both.   This complete vindication of
his character was as gratifying to his friends as it was mortifying to his opponents.   After three years he was succeeded in
the office by Benjamin Franklin, and took up his residence at
Wilmington, Delaware.   He was president of the Annapolis convention of delegates from several adjoining States, in 1786, to
consider a uniform system of commercial relations between the
States, out of which grew the convention to revise the Articles
of Confederation, in 1787.   He was a member of the latter
convention, and shared largely in its discussions.   Although
one of the wealthiest men in the Convention, he was one of the
most decided opponents of a property qualification for holding
office.   According to Hildreth, " he doubted the policy of in-
terweaving into a republican constitution a veneration for wealth.
It seemed improper that any man of merit should be subjected
to disabilities in a republic, where merit was understood to form
the great title to public trusts, honors, and rewards."   After
the promulgation of the constitution he exerted himself in every
way to secure its adoption.   The "Letters of Fabius," in its
advocacy, were written by him.

The last years of his life were passed at Wilmington.   Never
very robust in health, frequently taxed beyond his physical en-
durance, he retired from political life a number of years before
his death.   In person he has been described as " tall and spare,
his hair white as snow, his garb uniting with the severe simplicity of his sect a neatness and elegance peculiarly in keeping
with it."   He was loved and respected of all.   In social life, as a
conversationalist, his wide range of miscellaneous information,
his habitual elegance and eloquence of language, combined with
his sincerity of heart, made him exceedingly agreeable.   In his
sympathy he was practical as well as warm-hearted.   Upon the

death of his friend, George Read, in 1799, he modestly accompanied his expressions of sympathy with a deed for a valuable farm, with brick dwelling-house and other improvements, and one hundred and eighty acres of valuable wood land. All his public papers exhibit a supreme trust in an overruling Providence in the affairs of nations. In a letter to Doctor Nisbet, Doctor Rush alludes to him as "a gentleman who unites with the finest accomplishments of the man and the patriot a sacred regard to the doctrines and precepts of Christianity." He died at Wilmington, in 1808. Had he been more ambitious and less scrupulous in the use of means for his own advancement, he might have reached higher political position, but as it is, he has left a record of unimpeachable purity in private and public life, as well as of great influence and usefulness.

Chapter III.

OPENING OF THE COLLEGE—NISBET'S ADMINIS-
TRATION.

Meeting of Trustees at Carlisle—Seal—Oath of Office—Faculty—Dr. Nisbet Elected Principal—Induced to Accept—Arrival in America—Reception at
Carlisle—Prof. Davidson—Resignation of Dr. Nisbet—His Re-election—His Work—College Building
—The Barracks—Resources—State Aid—Subscriptions—Lottery—State Aid—First Commencement—
Requirements—Classes—Instruction—Regulations
Taney's Account—Fines—Building—Campus—West
College Burned Down—Re-built—Donations—Plan
of New Building—Death of Dr. Nisbet—His Character.

HE Board of Trustees, after its organization and
meetings held at the house of Doctor Rush, on
Second street, Philadelphia, and in the State-
house, met for the first time in Carlisle, in the
court-house, April 6, 1784. After assembling, before proceeding to business, they went in procession to the Episcopal church, where a sermon suitable to the occasion was delivered. Upon re-assembling, they were ably addressed by
President Dickinson, and immediately proceeded to the organization of the College. Ways and means were devised for
raising money, including a petition to the Legislature of the
State, addresses to religious bodies, a carefully prepared letter
to the Honorable William Bingham, in Europe, requesting him
to solicit aid there, and the preparation of subscription books

for circulation. A seal was also adopted, the device consisting of a Bible, a Telescope, and a Cap of Liberty, the two last placed over the first, with the motto: "*Pietate et doctrina tuta libertas.*" It was reported by Doctor Rush and President Dickinson, and, according to Doctor Rush, "the excellent sentiment" was suggested by the latter. The seals of colleges, in

their devices and mottoes, exhibit much of the spirit and purpose of their founders. The open Bibles of Harvard, Yale, and Amherst, and the red-cross of Brown, with the mottoes in harmony, indicate the connection of culture and religion. In the seal of Dickinson is introduced, in addition, the thought then uppermost, the guardianship of liberty just entrusted to independent America ; and that virtue and learning were to be its safeguards. Each member of the Board, in addition to his oath, as trustee, had taken and subscribed the "iron-clad" oath of that day, as follows: "'That we will be true and faithful to the Commonwealth of Pennsylvania, and that we will not, directly or indirectly, do any act or thing prejudicial or injurious to the Constitution or the Government thereof, as established by the Convention, and that the State of Pennsylvania is, and of right ought to be, a free, sovereign, and independent State, and that we do forever renounce and refuse all allegiance, subjec-

Rev. Charles Nisbet, D.D.
1784 – 1804.

FIRST PRESIDENT OF DICKINSON COLLEGE.

From Oil-Painting in College Chapel.

tion, or obedience to the King or Crown of Great Britain, and that we never have, since the Declaration of Independence, directly or indirectly, aided, assisted, or abetted, or in any wise countenanced the King of Great Britain, his generals, fleets, or armies, or their adherents, in their claims upon these United States, &c., &c."

Although the revenues from productive funds amounted to only £130 per annum, and they were almost without a building, it was thought advisable to commence operations, by organizing a faculty. Accordingly, the Reverend Charles Nisbet, D. D., of Montrose, Scotland, was elected Principal, and James Ross, A. M., well known as a classical scholar and author of a Latin Grammar, was elected Professor of Greek and Latin. Attention had been called to the former by Doctor Rush, who had made his acquaintance whilst a student in Edinburgh. The College of New Jersey had also been largely indebted to Doctor Rush for the acquisition of Doctor Witherspoon, as President, fifteen years before. At that time, Doctor Witherspoon, who at first declined the position, had suggested Doctor Nisbet "as the person of all his acquaintance the fittest for that office," although he was but thirty-one years of age. The interval, filled with the excitements and estrangements of the war, contained nothing calculated to render him less acceptable as the head of an American College; on the contrary, although thoroughly loyal to his Sovereign, he had been known, perhaps it might be said notorious, in his own country, as a fearless, outspoken friend of America, and champion of her rights, and he had suffered much for it. On one occasion, called upon to preach upon a public Fast, appointed by the Government, during the war, he selected Daniel v : 5—25, as his text. On a similar occasion, the members of the town council of Montrose, during the introductory remarks, left the church in a body, and the Doctor, stretching forth his hand

toward the vacant place, said with emphasis, as they withdrew :
"'The wicked flec when no man pursueth." Such a course
was not calculated to render him popular, and it was only the
respect for his great talents, preëminent learning and acknowledged piety and faithfulness that preserved him from serious
annoyance. He was the center of a circle of devoted friends,
including some of the most eminent men of Scotland. Among
the learned, he was known as a walking library. His excellent
social talent, his unrivaled wit and humor, combined with his
vast learning, caused his company to be courted. The principalship of a college in a new country, the plans of which were
on paper, and revenues in promises, it would seem, could hardly
be attractive enough, although presented with the greatest
unanimity, to draw him from his congenial literary surroundings
and assured position.

After most profound consideration, and without the encouragement of some of his most intimate and influential friends,
he finally concluded to cast in his lot with the Republicans of
the New World, with whom he had so deeply sympathized, and
for the defense of whose rights he had not feared to incur odium
at home. The picture that presented itself to his mind of the
"formative condition of America" in all respects, with the
"minds of its citizens free from the shackles of authority yielding more easily to reason," had considerable influence in pro-
ducing his decision, re-enforced as it was by the ardent, per-
sistent, and eloquent persuasions of his friend Doctor Rush,
with all the high coloring imparted to the prospects of the new
institution by his sanguine temperament. The natural caution
of Governor Dickinson, combined with his constant thought-
fulness of the comfort of others, at one time led him to dis-
courage Doctor Nisbet from accepting the position, by a frank
statement of his fears that the revolution in Pennsylvania politics, occasioned by the restoration of the right of suffrage to

the loyalists, was not favorable to the prospects of the College for State aid. The doctor, in a letter to the Earl of Buchan, clearly exhibits his views in regard to this turn in American politics in the following paragraph: "Perhaps the late Assembly of Pennsylvania have been too much in haste to obtain the reputation of being humane and merciful, by taking in those who have turned out themselves. If they had contented themselves with restoring the loyalists to their estate, but denied them the privilege of voting till they had passed a novitiate of ten or twelve years, the present confusion might have been avoided. * * * But imprudent counsels are common in all States."

On the 9th of June, 1785, after a voyage of forty-seven days from Greenock, he arrived in Philadelphia with his family, consisting of his wife and two sons and two daughters. During a delay of several weeks in Philadelphia, as the guest of Doctor Rush, he received every attention from the leading citizens, and was, upon the whole, very favorably impressed with the people and his prospects. He arrived at Carlisle on the 4th of July following. Upon information of his approach, a deputation of citizens and a troop of horse were dispatched to escort him into the town. On the following day the oath of office was administered, and he delivered a sermon from Acts VII, 22, upon the importance of the union of piety and learning, remarkable as the only sermon of his that was allowed to be printed. A Grammar School was already in successful operation under the charge of Professor Ross, assisted by Mr. Robert Johnson, tutor, and subsequently professor of Mathematics. At the first meeting of the Board of Trustees, after the arrival of Doctor Nisbet, Reverend Robert Davidson, D. D., was added to the faculty as professor of History, Geography, Chronology, Rhetoric, and Belles Letters, and a Mr. Jait was appointed " to teach the students to read and write the English language with elegance and propriety." Doctor Davidson was also, at the same time, settled as the pastor of the Presbyterian Church in Carlisle. He was a graduate of the University of Pennsylvania, and had been connected with it as an instructor, and, as will be seen, had an important share in conducting the College in its earlier years.

Before Dr. Nisbet had fairly entered upon his work, he was prostrated by a severe and protracted fever, together with several members of his family, and became so much discouraged by the effect of the climate upon his health, "especially of the great heats beyond the conception of any one who has not felt them," that, on the 18th of October, he resigned his position, resolved to return to Scotland. The trustess felt obliged to accept his resignation, though with great reluctance, and Professor Davidson was appointed Principal *pro tem.* Unable as well as unwilling to undertake a mid-winter voyage, Dr. Nisbet postponed his departure to the Spring, and in the meantime his health and spirits were so far restored, that he consented to a reëlection to his former position on the 10th of May following, and during his long subsequent connection with the College, his health was never seriously interrupted again.

In the faculty thus organized, Dr. Nisbet was not only *primus inter pares* in position, but also most decidedly in energy and amount of work. Connected with his position as principal was the chair of Moral Philosophy, but in order to bring the college curriculum nearer to his ideal, he delivered four co-ordinate courses of lectures on Moral Philosophy, Logic, Philsophy of the Mind, and Belles Lettres, and, upon the request of a class, added a fifth, on Systematic Theology, which extended over two years, and embraced four hundred and eighteen lectures, and is remarkable as probably the first course of lectures on systematic theology delivered in this country. He also filled the pulpit of the Presbyterian church alternately with Dr. Davidson, and with all, according to the request of the trustees, visited different parts of Pennsylvania and the adjoining States, to solicit money for and excite an interest in the institution, not a small matter at that time, when even postal communications were limited, and his journeys were for the most part made in the saddle.

Whilst the College seems thus to have been provided with an able and active faculty, the matter of buildings was apparently neglected. It is true that at the very earliest meetings of the trustees resolutions were passed for the purchase of grounds and the erection of buildings, but other matters, apparently more pressing and important, monopolized the attention and energy of the friends of the College, so that for nearly twenty years the exercises were conducted in a small two-story brick building, with four rooms, near the corner of Bedford street and Liberty alley, long known as the old College, replaced by a building employed for educational purposes by the borough. One cause for delay on this point was doubtless also the expectation entertained, when the College was located at Carlisle, that the government buildings adjoining the town would be obtainable, by donation or purchase, for the purposes of the College. In April, 1787, negotiations were entered into with Congress, through the Secretary of the Treasury, for their purchase, and subsequently a committee of the trustees was privately instructed to offer $20,000 for them, and political influence was brought to bear through the senators and representatives in Congress. It is said that Dr. Nisbet did occupy a portion of the buildings for a time, and that some of his lectures were delivered there, and that students were also accommodated in them for several years. It is perhaps not to be regretted that they did not become the permanent seat of the College, or the present more eligible site might not have been obtained.

The College was not only cramped by its limited accommodations, but even more by the slender support at its command. The aid expected from the State was tardily given. Public finances were as straightened as those of individuals. In 1786 the first grant was made, consisting of £500, in specie, and ten thousand acres of the unappropriated lands of the State. Many private individuals had made similar donations of unimproved land. However promising such property may have been for the remote future of the institution, it contributed little to its immediate support or growth. Under financial pressure, repeated authorizations were given for its sale by the trustees, but with practically no result. For the same reason, they formed a poor basis even for loans. The immediate expenses of the College were therefore met, in great part, by contributions. The latter, though not munificent in character, were, in many cases, liberal, especially for that day, and were from leading citizens in widely separated sections. In Philadelphia, the name of Robert Morris heads one list with £375, and among the other names are those of John Cadwallader, Thomas Willing, Charles Thompson, Benjamin Paschal, Edward Shippen, and John Ross. The report in regard to Baltimore, by Dr. Davidson, after a visit to that city, was that he had found the inhabitants well disposed toward the institution, and that they had subscribed with great generosity. Among the contributors was William Patterson, father of Madame Bonaparte. Even Richmond, Va., manifested its interest by substantial aid. The Chevalier de la Luzerne, Minister of France, paid $200 in specie.

Another expedient, however, of more doubtful morality now, but very usual then, in the form of a lottery, was resorted to. Other Colleges, at the time, as well benevolent and public enterprises of different kinds, had, under legislative sanction, employed the same method for pecuniary relief. In January,

1790, a lottery was advertised with much display, as authorized by the Legislature, "for raising the sum of $10,000 for erecting a City Hall in Philadelphia, and for the use of Dickinson College." The highest prize was $3,000, and the tickets four dollars each. After the scheme of prizes, the advertisement continued : "It is to be hoped that a lottery instituted for the purpose of improving the Capital of the State, and for promoting the interests of literature in its western parts will meet with encouragement from the public. The College of Carlisle has already exhibited very promising appearances of future usefulness to the State. Its central position, the respectable characters of its principal and professors, and the reputation it has already acquired for accurate and useful learning, render it an object worthy of general patronage in this and the neighboring States." Among the parties from whom it was announced tickets could be purchased in different localities, a very fair sprinkling of Reverends appears.

In 1791, the State came to the relief of the College, by a grant of £1,500, and subsequently, about 1796, an additional grant of $3,000 was made. In the midst of the severest financial embarrassments, the trustees did not fail, in some way, to provide the necessary educational appliances, as well as competent instructors. The expenditures for the library and philosophical apparatus, was more than liberal, in proportion to the resources.

In spite of all the difficulties and discouragements, the College assumed a very creditable rank as a literary institution. The first public commencement was held September 27, 1787, and the "first degree in Arts" was conferred on nine young men. There seems to have been no established course of study for the degree, as there was no established day for commencement. Neither were the students classified. When, in the opinion of the Faculty, a class could be advanced far enough for examination for graduation by a certain date, the fact was certified to the President of the Board of Trustees, and a meeting of that body was called by regular legal advertisement, and the day fixed for that class. These regulations prevailed as late as 1800. The second class, of eleven, was graduated on the 7th of May, 1788, a class of like number on the 3d of June, 1789, and of twelve on the 28th of September, 1790, whilst in 1791 there was no class; but on the 2d of May, 1792, the largest class was graduated that has gone out from the College, except that of 1858. The students were first classified in 1796, and a regular course of study was prescribed at the same time for graduation. But three classes, however, were formed, designated as Freshman, Junior, and Senior. The missing Sophomore link was not discovered until 1814. The curriculum in Latin and Greek was almost as extensive as at present, and the first year seems to have been almost entirely devoted to these languages and arithmetic. Lectures were almost exclusively employed in imparting instruction, where the subject permitted. Complaints in regard to this method of instruction were frequent. The Trustees, by resolution, repeatedly recommended more frequent exercises in recitation and examination, and at one time alleged that the institution was likely to suffer very much from the complaints of the students in regard to "the labor of writing out so great a number of lectures on the various branches of literature," and "that the dread of this circumstance had deterred many young men from coming to the College." They simply recommended that the labor should be lightened by abridging the amount of writing, but that the plan of education should in no degree be abridged.

There were many peculiarities of that period that gradually disappeared. The Latin Salutatory, which was considered the highest honor, and the Valedictory, next to it, were left to the decision of the class, until 1812, when the Trustees, discover-

ing that plan to be objectionable, imposed the duty of assigning
them upon the Faculty.   The account of Chief Justice Taney,
of the class of 1795, indicates the controlling influence of the
literary societies at that early day.   The selection, which was
by ballot, was generally decided upon the society line, the
literary society, which happened to be in numerical ascendency
in the class, even assuming to make the nominations for its members in the class, and generally, too, without hesitation, appro-
priating both of the honors.   According to the same authority,
the subjects of the orations of the graduates were not only
selected by Dr. Nisbet, but a skeleton, covering half a page of
small letter paper, by him, indicated the manner in which it
might be handled in any case.   The method employed for
securing attendance on recitations and prayers had, too, a different point of contact with the student.   The monitor of the
class, appointed weekly, called the roll upon every assembling
of the class, not, however, until the professor had taken his
chair.   Absentees were fined, at the discretion of the professor,
from 3d. to 6d.   All absences, fines, &c., were reported by the
monitor, at a weekly meeting of the professors, and all the
students held on Saturday morning, when fines were collected,
excuses heard, admonitions given, monitors appointed, &c., and
absence from this meeting, on the part of the student, was
punished by a fine of one eighth of a dollar.   "The moneys
arising from this source" were appropriated by the regulations
for fuel and for keeping the building in an orderly condition.
It might be feared that the physical comfort of students would,
in some degree, be in inverse ratio to their literary and moral
character, and yet this *argumentum ad crumenam* style of dealing with literary and moral delinquencies, so out of harmony
with our present notions, may have had some elements of efficiency in it that more modern devices lack.   Although the
commencements were held with great ceremony, and the Trus-

tees, Faculty, and students accompanied the graduating class in formal procession to the church, the exercises of the College were conducted in the "small, shabby building fronting on a dirty alley," as Taney narrates. The friends of the College were not indifferent to this feature. The Trustees kept constantly before themselves, and the community, the intention to have it remedied by resolving that it ought to be done, and by appointing committees to select a site, &c. After a grant of £1,500 by the Legislature, in 1791, such a committee was appointed to negotiate for the purchase of a lot in the borough, from the Penns, to build a "college house" upon, and also to prepare a plan, make estimates, &c.

It was not until 1798, however, that a committee on this subject found it possible or worth while to act. The present College campus, comprising a whole square of the town on its western limits, was then purchased of the Penns in fee for $150.* The ground was open at the time, and formed a part of what was called the "commons," under a prevalent impression that it had been set apart as open ground for the benefit of the town. Measures were at once taken looking to the erection of a building, and after great effort, it was in so far completed as to have been partially occupied by students, when it was totally destroyed by fire on the 3d of February, 1803. The friends of the College congratulated themselves that the library, apparatus, globes, charts, &c., had not yet been removed to it. The fire originated in one of the unfinished rooms, from ashes placed at a considerable distance from the building. A very high wind from the west prevailed at the time, carrying the charred shingles over the town beyond the Letort spring. Nothing seems to have prevented the conflagration of the whole town but a light fall of snow. Misfortunes of this character frequently develope a surprising amount of

---

* Deed recorded. Cumberland county, Book N, Vol. I, p. 327.

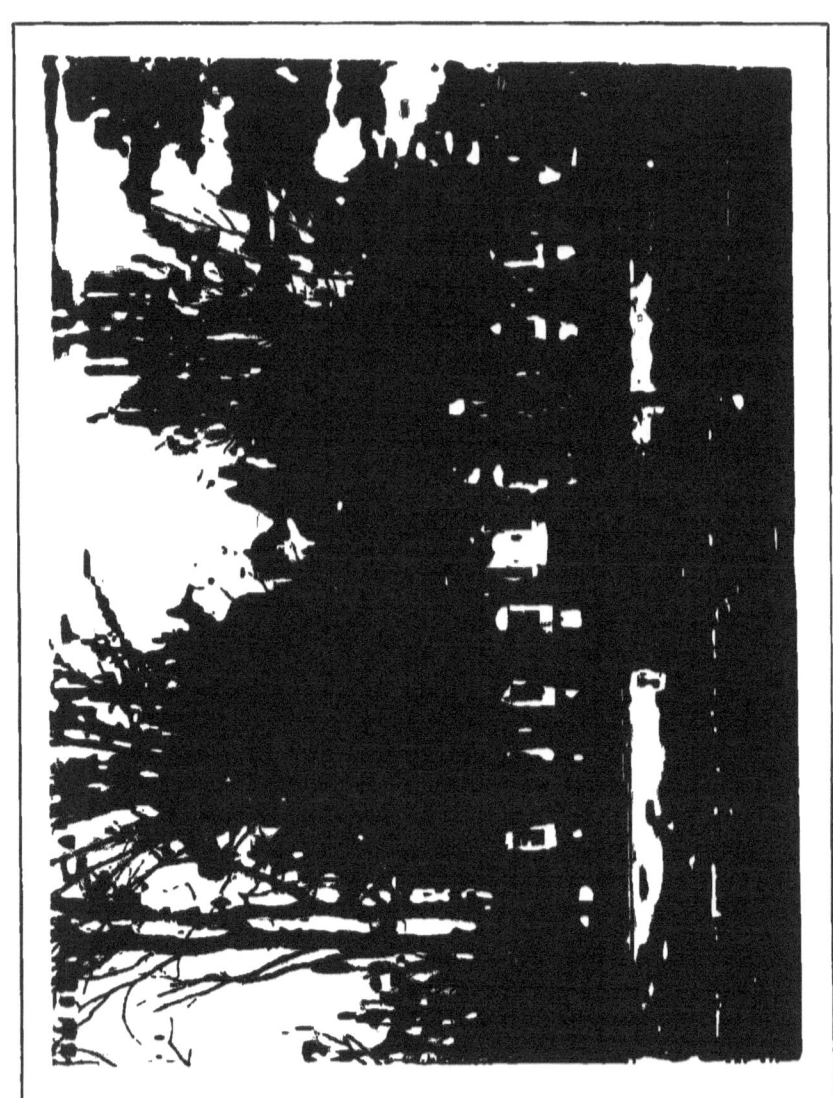

WEST COLLEGE.

latent vitality as well as unsuspected public spirit and ability. Judged by all the ordinary rules of diagnosis, the case of the institution struggling under a load of debt for the new building, would have been pronounced hopeless. But within twenty-four hours, a subscription for re-building was liberally filled in Carlisle, and a meeting of the trustees was called, at which, after setting forth the destruction of " the new and elegant building erected at the expense of many thousand dollars," they most vigorously entered upon measures for re-building. A committee was appointed to employ laborers to dig clay, make brick, and contract for other material. Contributions came in from unexpected sources. The destruction of the College was re garded as a national calamity. Political animosities were softened by it. The College had been notoriously in sympathy with the Adams administration in its trustees, its faculty, and its students. The latter had sent a letter expressive of their feelings to President Adams, to which he had given a very appreciative and fatherly reply.* But at this juncture, of seventeen members of Congress who contributed to the re-building of the College, all but one were Republicans, and even Jefferson received the committee courteously and gave $100. Count de la Lagune also headed a list with the State, aided with a loan of $6,000 upon unimproved lands of the College.

In August, 1803, the first stone of the new building was laid. The original intention was to construct it of brick. Plans, suggested by the Trustees, were submitted to Latrobe, the Government architect at Washington, who not only furnished the working plan, as finally adopted, but, fortunately, succeeded in having it carried out in stone. As represented in a letter from Judge Breckenridge, he argued that " either brick or stone would rust and acquire an appearance of age, which, however, would not be objectionable, as painters, in their drawings, give even

---

* Life and Works of John Adams, vol. IX, p. 204.

new buildings the rust of antiquity to make them venerable, and in large buildings, and of a public nature, it is especially becoming." But as to material, he was "decisively for stone, as proper for a large edifice, giving it the appearance of *strength.*" The entry was also thrown to the north, at his suggestion, and the door in the east end was not in the building, as originally constructed, but enlarged from a window, in 1834, at Doctor Durbin's suggestion. The length of the building is one hundred and fifty feet, and its breadth forty-five feet, and all the dimensions and the altitudes of the different stories and basement were carefully planned, with a view to harmonious architectural effect. It was not ready for occupancy until November, 1805, and then only in a partially finished condition internally. A donation from Doctor Rush, subsequently, was used in erecting partitions, and, in 1821, much remained to be done to completely adapt it to all the purposes for which it was intended. At present it contains a spacious and pleasant Chapel with a gallery, the Halls of the Belles Lettres and Union Philosophical Societies and two large rooms for their Libraries, the Reading-room, two Lecture-rooms, with offices for professors, a professor's residence, several rooms for students, besides ample accommocations for a students' boarding club in the basement.

Whilst the new building was in course of construction, the College met with its gravest misfortune in the death of Doctor Nisbet, January 18, 1804, after an illness of a few weeks, resulting from a heavy cold. He had just completed his sixty-eighth year. For nineteen years, through all the embarrassments and discouragements, and in spite of many deficiencies, he had given character to the young institution, and had attracted to it the sympathy and aid of friends of higher education as well as students. As a prominent factor in the teaching force, internally, and as a figure-head, externally, he had

almost constituted the institution.   At home in all branches of
human learning, he had his acquisitions so fully in hand, that
they were readily turned to account.   He was a fluent speaker,
and in the pulpit never used aids of any kind.   His imagina-
tion was lively, his wit keen, his sarcasm scathing, whilst he
was fearless and unreserved, at times, perhaps, needlessly so in
his expressions of opinion or of censure.   He had the use of at
least nine languages, and was at home in the whole range of classic
literature.   Some of his intellectual feats are incredible.   Whilst
in Europe, he was supposed to be one of the best Greek scholars
it contained.   His memory was as wonderful as his wit was
unequaled.   He could repeat whole books of Homer, the whole
of the Æneid, and is said to have often heard his recitations in
the classics without a text-book.   His life in America was not
a happy one.   His temperament was peculiar, and his ideal of
a College did not harmonize at all times with the views of the
trustees, and perhaps not with the demands of the country at
that time.   In discipline, he was generally regarded as too
lenient in the execution of law, but he relied upon his sarcasm,
which is said to have been the terror of disorderly students.
His methods of instruction were modeled after those of much
older institutions of very different character.   The disappoint-
ments encountered caused him at times to take a gloomy view of
American affairs, and combined with the impressions made by
the horrors of the French revolution, eventually imparted a
tinge of anti-republicanism to his sentiments.   This was prominent in his lectures to the students, and the young republicans
of the day simply omitted the offensive passages from their notes,
according to Taney, whilst their high regard for him as a man
restrained them from what would have been open rebellion with
any other professor.   The wonderful character of the man, so
out of joint with his surroundings, is apparent in the fact that
he retained his position without a question, and his death was

regarded as the greatest calamity that could have befallen the College. He lies buried in the old grave-yard of Carlisle. His monument bears a lengthy epitaph in Latin by Doctor Mason, one of his successors in office. His children were no discredit to so eminent a father. The only son that survived him, Alexander, was for many years a judge in Baltimore, and his daughters were married and filled highly respectable stations in life.

CHAPTER IV.

NISBET TO DURBIN—1804 TO 1833.

FACULTY—DR. DAVIDSON PRINCIPAL *pro tem.*—STATE AID—DECLINATION OF DR. MILLER—DR. ATWATER PRINCIPAL—APPARATUS AND LIBRARY—JUDGE COOPER PROFESSOR OF CHEMISTRY—SENIORS VOLUNTEER—DUEL—TRUSTEES AND DISCIPLINE—SUSPENSION OF THE COLLEGE—REORGANIZATION—STATE AID—DR. MASON PRINCIPAL—FACULTY—DR. NIELL PRINCIPAL—STATE AID—LEGISLATIVE INVESTIGATION—DR. HOW PRINCIPAL—DEFECTS IN THE CHARTER—WANT OF PROSPERITY.

F the faculty that surrounded Dr. Nisbet at the beginning, Dr. Davidson alone remained. He had been a faithful and invaluable aid. With more moderation and gentleness of disposition, and without any foreign peculiarities, he did much to harmonize jarring views and interests during the administration. Of the others, Professor Ross had resigned in 1792, and had been afterward appointed professor of languages in Marshall College, at Lancaster. He was succeeded by William Thompson, A. M. Professor Johnson, who had, in addition to Mathematics, given instruction for some time in Natural Philosophy, resigned in 1787, and was succeeded by

4

James McCormick, A. M., as tutor until 1792, and then as professor until 1814.   In addition, Charles Huston, A. B., afterward Judge of the Supreme Court of Pennsylvania, and Henry L. Davis, A. M., subsequently president of St. John's College, had filled positions as tutors.   Immediately after the death of Dr. Nisbet, Dr. Davidson was appointed principal *pro tem.*, a position he continued to hold for five years.   Although prominently named in connection with the principalship, and having the favorable opinion of Dr. Rush, the suggestion was not agreeable to him, and he finally resigned his position, in 1809, in order to devote himself wholly to the pastorate.   He had given instruction in languages, and had also for a long time filled the chair of Natural Philosophy, and is noticed more particularly in the sketch of the scientific department.   During his administration of the College, an additional grant of $4,000 was received from the State in 1806, of which a large amount was appropriated for the purchase of philosophical apparatus. Two classes were graduated in 1805, one in May and another in October.   In 1808 Dr. Samuel Miller was elected president. He had been urged by Dr. Rush as " a man of talents, learning, industry, and good temper, and a laudable ambition to be eminent and useful, and an American, who would not sport with our National government and character at the expense of the interests of the College."   This combination of excellencies, however, declined the honor, and in June, 1809, Rev. Jeremiah Atwater, D. D., President of Middlebury College, Vermont, was elected.   He left the position he had occupied for nine years, much to the regret of the friends of that institution, and with their best wishes.   In a farewell address delivered by him, he championed the usefulness of colleges.   After an able inaugural address, he took charge of the College.   Great stress was laid by the friends of the College upon his acquaintance with academic discipline, and a great improvement in this particular was claimed in the early part of his administration. Valuable additions were made to the library, and liberal sums were expended, through Dr. Rush, for the improvement of the apparatus. Several changes also occurred in the faculty. The building was divided into rooms for the accommodation of students, who were thus, for the first time, brought together in a separate building. Measures were taken to reduce the expenses of students. The number of students increased to seventy-seven in the first year. In 1811 the faculty was greatly strengthened by the election of Dr. Thomas Cooper, almost as eminent as a chemist as a jurist, to the chair of Chemistry and Mineralogy. In 1814, the Sophomore year was interpolated in the course. But difficulties, externally and internally, soon interfered with the continued prosperity of the College. The war had its effect. The greater part of the Senior class was in the volunteer ranks for the defense of Philadelphia, in 1814, and the degrees were conferred *in absentia.* A duel, in 1815, which resulted in the fall of a member of the Junior class, had a very depressing effect. The young man was an only son. Five other students, deeply involved, absconded. Difficulties in administration also set in. By a serious defect in the charter, that had been troublesome during Dr. Nisbet's administration, the Trustees and Faculty were joint administrators of discipline. The interference of the Trustees in the internal management of the College now became chronic. It culminated in June, 1815, in a resolution by which the principal and professors were required to report in writing, every Saturday, to the Secretary of the Board, every delinquent, with the judgment of the Faculty in each case, and the extent to which it had been executed. Within three months after this action, President Atwater, and Professors Cooper and Shaw resigned. The Rev. John McKnight was appointed president *pro tem.*, but in 1816 the operations of the College were suspended, after petitioning the State, without result, to modify the charter and to assume more immediate control of the College. .

In 1821 the Trustees proposed to re-convey to the State, for ready money, the lands granted it in 1786, and the securities received for such as had been sold. The proposition was accepted, and the College thus received $6,000 in cash, and $10,000 in five equal annual installments. The debts of the institution consumed $4,000 of the first sum, and $2,000 were employed in necessary repairs, and in completing West College internally, much as it is at present. A new policy was adopted of liberal salaries to professors of acknowledged talent and reputation, with the exclusive claim of the College upon their time. After several unsuccessful efforts to obtain a principal, the services of Rev. John M. Mason, D. D., of New York, were secured. Before accepting he had satisfied his mind by inquiries as to revenues, regulations, professorships. &c. An alumnus of Columbia College, he had, for a number of years, filled the office of provost of that institution. He brought with him a reputation for pulpit ability and eloquence second to none in America. Among his associates, Henry Vethake, A. M., was elected to the chair of Natural Philosophy and Mathematics, a gentleman of established reputation. Rev. Alexander McClelland, D. D., was elected professor of Belles Lettres and Philosophy of the Mind, with an extravagant endorsement by Dr. Mason, which was fully sustained by his marvelous rhetoric. The Rev. Joseph Spencer, A. M., was made professor of languages, with permission to make an engagement with the Episcopal congregation of Carlisle to supplement his salary. The Rev. Louis Mayer, of the German Reformed Church, by virtue of an arrangement with its synod, became professor of History and German Literature. Liberal appropriations were again made for the library, apparatus, and mineral cabinet.

Dr. Mason was inaugurated before a large concourse of people, Chief Justice Gibson administering the oath, and delivered an address of high character. The College thus officered, and greatly renewed as well in its Board of Trustees, entered upon its new career with much promise. The classes filled up, public confidence was restored. Owing, however, in great part to the impaired health of Dr. Mason, as well as the suspicions of political influences at work in the Board of Trustees, the numbers began to diminish, and in 1824 Dr. Mason resigned, to be succeeded by Rev. William Niell, D. D., the Faculty remaining essentially the same. In 1826 John W. Vethake, M. D., was added as Lecturer on Chemistry, a position filled the next year by John K. Finley, M. D., who subsequently was elected to the Chair of Chemistry. The Legislature, in the same year, renewed the appropriation of $3,000 per year for seven years. But attacks from the outside, divisions among the Trustees, disagreement between the latter and the Faculty, and eventually dissensions in the latter, prevented the proper development of the institution. Charges of political and sectarian influences in the Board of Trustees and Faculty became of such a character as to receive investigation by a committee of the Legislature, and acquittal by the latter did not neutralize the effect of the notoriety, nor allay the unpleasant feelings generated. The mixed government of the Trustees and Faculty was also fatal to good order.

In 1829, Dr. Neill resigned, together with the whole faculty. Professor Spencer was appointed Principal *pro tem.*

In January, 1830, Reverend Samuel B. How, D D., was elected, and inducted into office March 30. A new faculty was organized, consisting of Reverend Alexander McFarlane, A. M., Professor of Mathematics, Charles D. Cleaveland, A. M., Professor of Languages, and Henry D. Rogers, A. M., Professor of Chemistry and Natural Philosophy. Every effort was made to recover the lost ground. The Trustees issued a pamphlet of nearly one hundred closely printed pages explanatory of the history from 1821 to 1830, which, however, was hardly calculated to produce a good effect. A new course of study was made out, and fuller statutes for the government of the College. The Alumni Association issued an address full of encouragement. Among the signatures of the committee, was that of James Buchanan. At the commencement of 1830, the procession moved to the church escorted by a troop of horse and several companies of volunteers. The Alumni oration was delivered by William Price, Esq., of Hagerstown, Maryland, and the question : Would it be expedient for the United States to establish a National University? was discussed by Benjamin Patten, Esq., and Honorable John Reed. The old organic defect, however, soon made its presence felt in new internal difficulties. The Trustees at last awake to the real difficulty too late, resolved to petition the Legislature to amend the charter so as to make the President of the College, *ex-officio*, a member of the board, and to commit the discipline of the College entirely into the hands of the Faculty, with exception of an appeal to the Trustees in case of expulsion, a practically nominal exception, whilst the power to dismiss was to be final with the Faculty. But the remedy was proposed too late, and in March, 1832, the Trustees felt constrained to consider the question of suspending the operations of the College, although one installment of the appropriation by the State still remained available.

REV. JOHN P. DURBIN, D. D.

President of Dickinson College.

1833–1845.

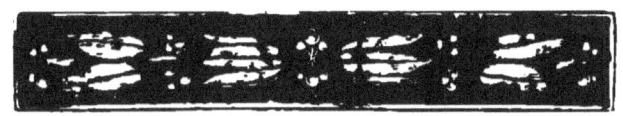

Chapter V.

REORGANIZATION UNDER THE METHODIST EPISCOPAL CHURCH—ADMINISTRATIONS OF DR. DURBIN, DR. EMORY, AND DR. PECK—1833-1852.

Higher Education in the Methodist Church—Transfer of Dickinson Suggested—Trustees Favorable—College Undenominational—Grounds for Transfer—Mode of Transfer—Unanimity of Action—New Control—Election of Dr. Durbin—Grammar School.—Change of Charter—Organization of a Faculty—Character of the First Faculty—South and East Colleges—Changes in the Faculty—Resignation of Dr. Durbin—Election of Dr. Emory—Elective Course—Death of Dr. Emory—Changes in the Faculty—Administration of Dr. Peck—Scholarship Endowment Plan.

T this juncture the educational movement in the Methodist Episcopal Church had fairly set in, or it may be said, was earnestly revived. Its earlier efforts toward the establishment of Cokesbury College, between 1785 and 1795, near Baltimore, although at first promising success, finally proved so fruitless that, for a quarter of a century, the field of higher education was neglected by that church. But a few years previous to the date reached in the history of Dickinson, Augusta College, in Kentucky, had been established by it, and Wesleyan University, in Connecticut, was just inaugurated. The old Baltimore Conference had been considering the question of the establishment

of a college for several years. On the 12th of March, 1833, a
special meeting of the Trustees of the College was called to
consider a letter of Reverend Edwin Dorsey, stating that the
Baltimore Conference had appointed a committee to consider
the propriety of establishing a college within its bounds, and
inquiring whether Dickinson College could be obtained by that
church, for that purpose, and on what conditions. The suggestion of a transfer to the Methodist Church met with favor,
and a general meeting of the Trustees was called, by resolution, for the 18th of April, at which time a committee of the
Baltimore Conference met with that body, and laid before it
the resolutions of their Conference, expressive of its willingness to embrace the opportunity to secure the institution, and
to assume the accompanying obligations to support it, and inquiring whether the transfer could be made. The Philadelphia
Conference, in the meantime, became associated with the Baltimore Conference in the enterprise, and was equally recognized by the Trustees in the matter.

A committee of the Trustees, after conferring with this committee, made a report favorable to the proposed arrangement.
Among the reasons assigned was : "That those colleges in the
United States that have been conducted by, or under the patronage of, some prominent Christian sect, have been more
flourishing in their operations, and more useful in their influence, than others that have not had these advantages." Up to
this time the College had been regarded as under the control of
the Presbyterian Church. Undoubtedly, at its origin, and
throughout its whole history, that church was looked to for its
main support in money and patronage, but the Board of
Trustees was a joint one, of different denominations, and different church organizations were asked to coöperate, as such,
in its support. In later years, one of the charges before the
legislative committee was the election of trustees in such a way

as to secure Presbyterian control. The professor of languages was, at the time, not only an Episcopalian, but sustained the same relation to that church, in Carlisle, that Doctors David- son and Nisbet had to the Presbyterian. Professor Mayer was of the German Reformed Church. The College, at its trans- fer, cannot, therefore, be regarded as a gift or surrender from the Presbyterian, or any other denomination, to the Methodist Church. Had it been recognized then as fully as a Presbyterian college, as it is now as a Methodist institution, it may be re- garded as doubtful whether it would have been so readily abandoned by that denomination. The transfer of this large public interest, to the control of the Methodist Church was, in the language of the Trustees, regarded as a proper expedient for the effectual and direct promotion of the original design of the founders of the College, that church formally declaring its willingness and intention to assume it, and obligating itself to properly support it as a college. A committee, appointed by the Conferences, with plenary powers to arrange prelimina- ries for its proper transfer and control, if they deemed it wise, after carefully considering the subject, in sessions running through a week, reached an affirmative decision. The mode of transfer was very deliberately considered in all its legal as- pects, and finally it was regarded as most advisable that it should be accomplished by the gradual resignation of the trustees then in office, and the election, in their stead, of those provisionally appointed by the Conferences.

The Conferences thus acquired the exclusive right to the possession of the grounds, buildings, fixtures, apparatus, libra- ries, &c., for the purposes of a literary institution. The action was unanimous on the part of the trustees present, and absent members were notified of the action of the Board, and requested to coöperate, and the body adjourned to meet on the 6th of June, after having ordered that, in the meantime, a circular letter should be sent, at least three weeks before the date of the meeting, to each member of the Board, embodying its action, and stating that an election for members of the Board would take place at the meeting. At that meeting, a committee of the Conferences, with Bishop Emory as chairman, was introduced to the Board of Trustees, and after a short conference, retired. The vacancies in the Board of Trustees were, thereupon, increased to eighteen, by resignations, and individuals nominated by the committee were elected in their stead. The Board then organized anew, by the election of Bishop Emory as President, whose careful judgment is visible in all the preliminary proceedings, and the renewal of the Board was completed during the year. Thus the transfer was made openly, with the utmost deliberation, and after the fullest consideration of all the interests and responsibilities involved on both sides, with the utmost harmony of feeling on the part of all concerned, and with the sole view to promote the public good.

The new Board proceeded at once to carry out the programme. The last installment of $3,000 of the State appropriation, together with some bank stock, was more than sufficient to pay the debts of the institution, and the surplus was expended in repairs and the improvement of the grounds. It is singular that the latter should have been neglected so long, susceptible as they have proved to be, of being rendered highly attractive at so little expense. To be sure, among the very earliest resolutions of the Trustees was one that upon a certain day trees would be planted, &c., and directing advertisement of the fact, and calling upon the citizens to assist. But, like many other good resolutions, it came to naught. The grounds were now, however, leveled, avenues were laid out, trees planted, and a substantial stone fence, mounted with an ornamental palisade, was placed on the south and east sides. Little else was necessary, but to allow development; and after the lapse of half a

century, the unrivaled beauty of the campus testifies to the
taste, as well as thoughtful care, that projected its plans so far
into the future. Agents were appointed by the Conferences to
solicit subscriptions; addresses were issued to the public. Although, at the recommendation of the Conferences, the Trustees
had resolved not to open the College until an endowment of
$45,000 had been subscribed, they gave evidence of their
faith, as well as purpose, by electing Reverend John P. Durbin,
D. D., editor of the *Christian Advocate*, Principal and Professor of Moral Science, with the notification that the College
would not open until the following May.

A grammar school was, however, organized at once, under
the charge of Alexander F. Dobb, which, at the close of the
year, had fifty pupils. In September Dr. Durbin signified his
acceptance, and met with the Board. Six professorships were
agreed upon, and several professors were provisionally elected.
A department of law was also established, under the care of
Judge Reed, limited to the fees of the students for its support.
A committee was also appointed, which secured from the
Legislature important changes in the charter, making the Principal *ex officio* President of the Board of Trustees, and giving
the final decision, in all cases of discipline, to the Faculty,
without appeal to the Trustees, except in case of expulsion, a
merely nominal exception, whilst the equivalent penalty of
dismission was left with the Faculty. At the next meeting, in
May, 1834, the reports of the agents of the conferences exhibited subscriptions amounting to $48,000, and it was resolved
to open the College in the following September. In that
month the Faculty was organized. Dr. Durbin was inducted
into office, and delivered a very able address, setting forth the
views and intentions of those in control. Professor Caldwell,
who had been previously elected, was assigned to the chair of
the Exact Sciences, and Rev. Robert Emory was elected Pro-

fessor of Ancient Languages. Both took the oath of office as professors, and delivered addresses suitable to the occasion. Other professorships were filled by election, and the College opened. Thus the College entered upon its second half century, not only with the profit of the experience of fifty years, with amended charter, with repaired buildings, with beautified grounds, but with new forces, new impulses at work. For the first time in its history, it was avowedly and unmistakably denominational in its controlling body. The professorship of Natural Sciences, which was vacant by the declination of the professor-elect, was filled, in July, 1835, by the election of John M. Keagy, M. D.; and upon his resignation, a year afterward, by reason of ill health, William H. Allen, A. M., of Augusta, Maine, was elected Lecturer on Natural Science and Instructor in Modern Languages for one year. During the year 1836, the professor-elect of Mathematics announced his declination of the position, and Rev. John M'Clintock, A. M., was engaged to teach these branches, *ad interim*, and at the meeting of the Trustees in 1837, he was elected to the professorship, and Dr. Allen, at the same time, to that of Natural Science. The permanent organization of the first faculty was thus complete.

It has always been regarded as fortunate that the re-organized College had the services of these men. It may be said, that Dr. Durbin alone brought to the institution an established reputation. As a preacher, he was widely known. He had been Chaplain of the United States Senate. His inexplicable eloquence had made him a power wherever he was announced to appear. He had declined a professorship in Wesleyan University. He left the most influential editorial chair of the denomination to assume charge of this high educational trust. As the organizing and directing head of such an enterprise, and as a college administrator, he has perhaps never been equaled.

According to the polity of American Colleges, especially of the smaller ones, a President is so essential as a figure head and financial agent, as well as administrator and instructor, that they often suffer for want of the combination of these qualities in a high degree in one individual, and so long as the system continues as it is, there will be a demand for men that are but seldom met with. A graduate of a college, and subsequently a professor of languages in Augusta College, he was, also, not a novice in the peculiarities of college life. His varied acquisitions and tastes put him in full sympathy with all branches of human learning. Every department and every interest of the College felt the touch of his attention. Revised statutes, new courses of study, new buildings, endowment, increase of students, &c., were all subjects of his constant consideration.

In the following paragraph, from the pen of Dr. W. H. Allen, one of his colleagues, his character as the presiding officer of the College is condensed :

" He was a man of tact, courteous, prudent, cautious, wise. He carried his measures in faculty meetings by a marked respect for his colleagues and deference to their opinions, while he adroitly molded their opinions to the shape of his own by modest suggestions and a certain recondite influence, which was perceived only by its effects. His well known devotion to the interests of the College gave weight to his recommendations to the Trustees, and they always assented to his propositions. In the presence of his classes, Durbin did not merely hear recitations * * * he gave instruction. He placed his own mind in electric communication with the minds of his students."

The other members of the Faculty were young men, and as was natural, not widely known in the Church, and two of them from a section widely distant from the College. For the same reason they were without special reputation in the departments to which they had been assigned ; they doubtless had predelic-

tions for them, but they had not as yet selected the fields of
their special exertions.

The mathematics were soon abandoned by Professor M'Clintock for the more congenial study of languages and metaphys
ics.   However congenial scientific studies were to Professor
Allen, and in spite of his eminent success as a teacher in that
department, he subsequently acquired his greatest reputation
and influence outside of them.   Emory hesitated between the
professor's chair and the pastorate, with his decision in favor of
the latter, until called to the presidency of the College, and
had barely become fixed in purpose, and had but begun to de-
monstrate fully the wonderful elements of his character, when
he was removed by death.   Caldwell, too, was stricken down
without opportunity to display his ripened ability.   But they
all seem to have brought to the College the capital elements of
success.   They all possessed natural ability of the highest, in
some cases unusual, order.   If not specialists, they all had the
broad basis of a thorough liberal culture.   Emory had graduated with the honors at Columbia College, Caldwell and Allen
were graduates of Bowdoin, and M'Clintock of the University
of Pennsylvania.   They were studious and conscientious, as
well as enthusiastic in their devotion to their work.   However,
diverse their fields of labor, they recognized a common object
in the advancement of the interests of the College.   In a short
time they not only established reputations for themselves, but
gave to the institution prominence, and a warm place in the
affections and interest of the Church.   They live, deservedly,
not only in the memories of the graduates that passed out from
beneath their instruction, but as well in the grateful recollection
of the Church.   It must not, however, be overlooked, that the
strength of their maturer years, and great usefulness in their
subsequent fields of labor, were as much a contribution of the
College to the Church as were those who were trained by them.

The scholastic leisure, and the associations and opportunities of college life formed an atmosphere necessary to their full, symmetrical development. There were, too, it is true, many conditions peculiarly favorable to the success and development of this first faculty, as well as unusual obstacles to be overcome, and reasons why it should hold a more decided lodgment in the memory of the Church than any subsequent one. It had all the inspiration of the awakening impulses of the Church, in regard to higher education; colleges were then novel enterprises in the Church, as well as grand ones. Neither was it trammeled by traditions, nor depressed by contrasts with a preceding golden age, however earnest its efforts. The Church, although it did not measure up to the promises made or expectations formed, was earnest in its efforts, and, according to its ability, perhaps did more for the College than at any other period. The trustees, too, selected by the conferences, had a similar inspiration, and were under a sense of great responsibility. This Faculty has been sketched incidentally by Dr. Crooks, in his Life of M'Clintock, as only could be done by one who knew them all intimately. Emory and M'Clintock were especially intimate. "Each was the other's *alter ego.* They were alike and yet unlike. Both were affectionate, buoyant, and full of the inspirations of hope. In Emory the logical faculty predominated over all others, and gave to his mind a judicial exactness. M'Clintock's equally great logical force was swayed by a mercurial temperament, and a lively fancy. In the acquisition of knowledge the latter was ardent, and swift as the wind, but in the eagerness of the pursuit, oblivious of a prudent self-care. His associate, though equally ardent, moved with a more deliberate step. Of the two, Robert Emory was, however, the first to wear himself out : he died before the promise of his earlier years was more than partly fulfilled. Professor Allen created perpetual surprises by his great versatility. He

EAST COLLEGE.

passed from department to department with a facility that made
one doubt which was the one he most preferred. Professor
Caldwell's high moral character impressed every one who came
near him. New England ruggedness was in him, tempered by
a tender moral sensibility."

Although the subscriptions upon which the College was
opened were not fully realized, and the Church seemed to come
tardily up to the fulfillment of its promises in regard to the
College, owing largely to the great financial depression that set
in, South College was purchased in 1835, for Grammar School
purposes, with an ample lot ninety feet by two hundred and
forty feet, separated from the Campus by Main street. It was
subsequently burned down and re-built, and is at present occupied exclusively by the scientific department and college library.
In 1836, East College was erected of native limestone on the
usual parallelopiped model of college dormitories. It is one
hundred and thirty feet long by thirty-two feet broad and four
stories high, and contains, besides three lecture-rooms with professors' offices attached, and rooms for eighty students, the residence of the President, and accommodations for a students'
boarding-club. Although it may not be considered attractive in
appearance in comparison with the more modern extravagant
specimens of college architecture, it is about up to the average
type of college dormitory buildings in external appearance,
and internal finish and accommodation. Money was also freely
expended for the library and apparatus. At times it was found
necessary to incur debt and financial responsibility, but the faith
in the success of the enterprise, and in the earnestness and
liberality of the Church does not seem to have been misplaced.
In 1840, Professor Emory resigned the chair of Ancient Languages to enter the pastorate, much to the regret of all connected with the College, and Professor M'Clintock was transferred to the vacant chair. At the same time, Colonel Thomas

E. Sudler, of St. John's College, was unanimously elected Professor of Mathematics, and accepted the position, although he
had declined that chair as well as that of Natural Science ten-
dered him immediately after the re-organization. Leave of
absence was also granted Dr. Durbin to visit Europe. During
his absence, in 1842, Robert Emory was re-called to the College
as President *pro tem*.

In 1845, Dr. Durbin resigned and returned to the pastorate
in Philadelphia. This step was taken by reason of "permanent
interests of his children and family, which required his presence
for some time in Philadelphia," and he assured the Trustees that
his resignation was wholly on account of these private interests
that he could not neglect, and that he wished it might be otherwise. At the same meeting, Rev. Robert Emory, A. M.,
was elected his successor, and signified his acceptance, and
Spencer F. Baird, of the class of 1840, was elected Professor
of Natural History and Curator of the Museum. The following year showed an increase in the number of students, and
at its close in 1846, Dr. George R. Crooks, of the class of
1840, who had had charge of the preparatory school, was added
to the Faculty as Adjunct-Professor of Languages. A fine and
thorough scholar, he was the collaborator of M'Clintock in
the preparation of a series of text-books in Latin and Greek
that enjoyed a wide popularity, and his subsequent career as
editor and author fully realized the promise of his earlier life at
Dickinson. The substitution of modern languages for other
studies, without affecting the graduation of the student was also
permitted, a plan that was more fully adopted a year afterward.

The health of Professor Caldwell had been precarious for
several years, and during 1847, Dr. Emory, after an attack of
hemorrhage of the lungs, went to the West Indies by medical
advice. The college work was distributed, as best it could be,
among the Faculty. At the meeting of the Trustees in July,

5

1848, it fell to the lot of Dr. Allen, as acting president, to com-
municate the most serious loss the institution had experienced
since its re-organization. Emory and Caldwell had passed away,
and Professors M'Clintock and Crooks had signified their intention to resign ; the former called by the Church to the editor-
ship of its leading periodical. He was led the more cheerfully
to accept the new position by reason of the sad changes that
had deprived him of his most intimate friends at the College,
and also by reason of a restiveness under a restraint he felt imposed upon the free expression of his unequivocal anti-slavery
sentiments. He had passed through a trial for his life in the
dock with twenty negroes, because of his courageous friendship
for them, and although acquitted not only by the court but by
the friends of the College, the students, and the intelligent
public, he was still M'Clintock the " abolitionist," though prudent in his expression of opinions out of consideration for the
interests of the College with which he was identified.

In 1848, Dr. Jesse T. Peck was elected President ; Professor
Allen was transferred to the chair of English Literature and
Philosophy, and Professor Baird to that of Natural Science.
The chairs of Mathematics and Ancient Languages were filled,
respectively, by Messrs. Otis H. Tiffanny and James W. Marshall, as adjunct professors, both being recent graduates of the
College. The dissolution of the first Faculty thus begun by
death and resignations, was completed in 1850, by the resignation of Dr. Allen, to assume the presidency of Girard College,
and of Professor Baird to enter upon the post of Assistant
Secretary of the Smithsonian Institution, with special charge
of the National Museum.

If the administration of Dr. Emory is to be regarded as
one of strict discipline, that of Dr. Peck was one of moral
suasion and of mild disciplinary expedients. One of his colleagues says of him, that " he was a man of commanding pres-

ence, had a good voice, was a reputable preacher, but he had not received a collegiate education, and his want of acquaintance with what might be termed the unwritten law of Colleges, subjected him to numerous embarrassments. He was a man of large heart, genial, sincere, friendly, and confiding." The chair of English Literature was filled by the election of Reverend H. M. Johnson, then Professor of Ancient Languages in Ohio Wesleyan University, that of Natural Science by the election of Reverend Erastus Wentworth, D. D., for four years previous, and at the time, President of McKendree College, Illinois, and James W. Marshall was promoted to the Professorship of Ancient Languages.

In 1851 Professor Sudler resigned, and Rev. O. H. Tiffany, the adjunct professor for four years, was elected his successor. At the same time Dr. Peck resigned the presidency, to take effect at the end of the ensuing year, with the determination to devote himself to the more congenial work of the pastorate. One of the most far-reaching measures in importance, was then also first presented to the notice of the trustees, in a communication from Professor Johnson, in regard to the production of an endowment fund by the sale of cheap scholarships, and an extra meeting of the Trustees was held in February, 1852, to consider a more detailed plan wrought out by Professor Johnson in the meantime.

CHAPTER VI.

PROGRESS OF THE COLLEGE—1852—ADMINISTRATIONS OF DR. COLLINS AND DR. JOHNSON.

ELECTION OF DR. COLLINS—PROSPERITY—CHARACTER OF DR. COLLINS—THE FACULTY—MARKS OF PROGRESS—CHANGES IN THE FACULTY—EFFECT OF THE WAR—HASTY GRADUATION—TREATMENT BY THE INVADERS—PEACE—DEATH OF PROFESSOR WILSON—ELECTIVE COURSES—CENTENNARY ENDOWMENT—DEATH OF DR. JOHNSON—HIS CHARACTER—HIS SUCCESSORS.

T the regular Annual Meeting, July 7, 1852, Dr. Peck persisted in his determination to withdraw from the College, and Rev. Charles Collins, D. D., President of Emory and Henry College, Va., was unanimously elected President. With this election the College entered upon an administration of marked character, to which the preceding four years formed the transition from the old. In it the College, judged by very usual criteria, enjoyed the highest prosperity it had as yet attained. The number of students reached its maximum, and the College demonstrated its capacity for the accommodation of at least two hundred and fifty students. The plans for the endowment fund succeeded so far as to give it an income, at times, above the ordinary current expenses, to be applied to general repairs and improvements. The scholarship of the graduates, there is no reason to believe, fell below that of any previous period. No better evidence of this fact can be given than that they are beginning frequently, by mistake, to be adopted by the grad-

uates of the Augustan age, in their chronicles of it. The
period, too, was, perhaps to a greater degree than any preceding one, a test of administrative ability. Difficulties in college administration increase, according to a very rapid ratio,
with numbers. The well-regulated-family plan receives a
severe strain. But besides, it succeeded an unsuccessful attempt at discipline by mild methods, which had left its tendencies, as well as its traditions, among the students. As
college generations move off of the stage rapidly, college history has a tendency to repeat itself rapidly. It is not singular
that Dr. Collins, who brought order out of this chaos, and re-
established the reign of college law, should have acquired the
reputation of a rigid disciplinarian. But those who knew him
most intimately then, and those who were thrown into association with him in post-graduate life, found beneath the dignified,
perhaps forbidding, exterior, as warm-hearted, sympathetic,
and genial a man as ever college president presented. Prompt
in decision, and in action, he impressed the students as equally
without weakness for their applause, or fear or hesitation in the
discharge of any duty, however irksome or unpleasant, whilst
he was so clear in his statements, that there was no room for
misunderstandings. Added to these qualities, which made
him, unquestionably, the man for the hour, were a dignified
and commanding presence, ripe scholarship, indomitable
energy and will, a deep interest in the cause of education, fine
business qualifications, all superintended by vigorous common
sense. He, perhaps, came as near to that bundle of somewhat incompatible qualifications embraced in the ideal college
president, as any one who has had charge of old Dickinson,
with the exception of the remarkable man who reorganized it
under its new control.

The Faculty associated with him, although wanting in some
of the elements of brilliancy found in the first Faculty, was

an effective working Faculty. The disciplinary details of a
large and growing institution absorb time and energy that
might otherwise manifest themselves in greater intellectual influence. The Professor of Ancient Languages, James W. Marshall, A. M., had graduated in the class of 1848, with high
distinction, and owed his position mainly to the high estimate
of his abilities and acquirements formed by Dr. M'Clintock.
He was an earnest, pains-taking, conscientious teacher, with an
influence for good upon the students at every point of contact
with them. He resigned his position in 1862, and was appointed consul to Leeds, England, and subsequently became
First Assistant Postmaster General during General Grant's administration. The chair of Mathematics was filled by Rev.
Otis H. Tiffany, who, without having made the study of
mathematics a specialty, had the faculty of instructing as far as
the course was carried, an ability that is perhaps more frequently wanting in mathematical instructors than others. As
a pulpit orator and lecturer, and on the higher political ros-
trum, he was popular, and stepped naturally out of the College
into the field of the pastorate, where he has filled some of the
most prominent pulpits of the denomination. The Professor
of Natural Science, Rev. Erastus Wentworth, was a man of no
ordinary character. If he did not devote himself exclusively
to the work of the department, and hardly maintained its already well-established character, he fully filled it according to
the prevalent notions in regard to the place and character of
natural science in a college curriculum. As a preacher, he
possessed a unique power. As a magazine writer, he wielded
a graceful and vigorous pen. As a professor, he may be said
to have been decidedly popular. In English Literature and
Philosophy, Professor Johnson was unsurpassed as a suggestive
and stimulating teacher. He, to a greater extent than any
other member of the faculty, taught by subjects, instead of by

pages of text-book: at one time requiring ten pages, at another forty pages, and the student, unused to this diminuendo and crescendo style of assigning recitations, was often loud in his complaints. But looking back over more than a quarter of a century intervening, the intelligent teacher appears in his apparent want of rule or method. Whilst he could hardly be said to have been popular with the students, he had what he valued more, their quiet respect and confidence in his ability as a teacher. Keen in wit and sarcasm, he at times, perhaps, impaired his influence for good by yielding to the temptation to wield it too unsparingly against some unfortunate, not, however, for the purpose of display, for which the elevation of the professor's chair affords so fine an opportunity, but from sheer inability to resist the impulse. Withal, he was kind in disposition, uniformly gentlemanly in his bearing, and earnestly interested in every young man entrusted to his care. As professor, he considered deeply the general interests of the College. The endowment plan, as has been stated, was his suggestion, and the plan as finally adopted in detail was essentially his work. It was natural that he should succeed to the administration of the College, upon the resignation of Dr. Collins, in 1860. Instruction in the modern languages was well provided for, at first under the care of Professor Charles E. Blumenthal, A. M., M. D., and subsequently under Professor Alexander J. Schem, since so well known as Assistant Superintendent of Schools in New York city, and writer on a variety of subjects.

The resignation of Dr. Collins was due to the demands of a large and growing family, which the income from the position was inadequate properly to support. He immediately assumed charge of the Tennessee Female College, at Memphis, which he administered successfully and profitably for a number of years. He died at Memphis. The introduction of the scholarship plan of endowment, extensive repairs, and improvements of East College, the purchase of the telescope, and the fitting up of the observatory, and many minor evidences of progress had marked the administration. Several changes had occurred in the Faculty. In 1854, Professor Wentworth, with one of the graduates of that year, Rev. Otis Gibson, at the call of the Church, engaged in missionary work in China. William C. Wilson, A. M., of the class of 1850, was put in charge of the department, as lecturer on Natural Science. He had been engaged in teaching in a classical school in Chester county, and brought to the position fine promise of success. Upon the retirement of Professor Tiffany, in 1857, Rev. William L. Boswell, A. M., of the class of 1848, and a successful Professor of Ancient Languages in Genesee College, was elected Professor of Mathematics, and, in 1860, was transferred to the chair of Greek and German, and Samuel D. Hillman, A. M., of the class of 1850, who had previously been principal of the Grammar School, was elected Professor of Mathematics. The work of the chair of English Literature and Philosophy, after the election of Dr. Johnson to the presidency of the College was distributed among the Faculty, and upon the retirement of Professor Marshall, in 1862, John K. Stayman, A. M., of the class of 1841, first elected adjunct-professor in 1861, was elected Professor of Latin and French.

For several years previous to the election of Dr. Johnson, the advancing tide of civil war had begun to make itself felt in the College, situated so near the border, and drawing its patronage equally from both sections. At the first outbreak of hostilities the number of students was rapidly diminished, and, almost at the same time, the College was called upon to face the new embarrassment of a diminished revenue, by the failure in productiveness of a large part of its invested endowment fund, which remained in this condition during the greater portion of the war. Notwithstanding all the discouraging and depressing circumstances of the period of the war, this Faculty carried on the regular work of the College without interruption. Each year, at the regular time, a class went forth with the honors of the College, that of 1863, however, rather hastily from the College chapel at an early hour on Commencement Day, the usual formalities being dispensed with, by reason of the rumored near approach of the invading army. Upon the occupation of the borough a few days afterward, not only the buildings and other property of the College were preserved from injury, but even the beautiful Campus was left unmarred by the careful occupancy of the troops in gray, the loyalty of many of them to their Alma Mater proving a more unchangeable passion than that to the flag of their country. When shells were distributed freely afterward, however, in an attack by Fitz Hugh Lee, several fell within the grounds, one entered the President's lecture-room and another passed through the roof of South College

With the return of peace, new hope sprung up for the College, although its finances seemed hopelessly embarrassed. On the 2d of March, 1865, with the prospect of early reëstablishment of the government he had so longed to see, Professor Wilson passed quietly away. At the ensuing meeting of the trustees, in June, the place thus made vacant was filled by the election of Charles F. Himes, of the class of 1855, then resident in Germany, and for several years previously Professor of Mathematics in Troy University. The resignation of Professor Boswell occurred at the same time. During the following year, owing to the declination of the gentleman elected to the vacancy, Rev. S. L. Bowman, of the class of 1855, was temporarily appointed Professor of Greek and Hebrew, and at the ensuing meeting of the trustees, was duly elected professor. At the same time the elective Biblical course of study was given greater prominence, and an elective Scientific course was established, extending to the Junior and Senior years. Measures were also perfected for increasing the endowment fund, by presenting the claims of the College during the centennial of American Methodism, in 1866. As a result, $100,000 were added to the productive funds.

Everything seemed to promise well, when, on the 5th of April, 1868, President Johnson was removed by death, after a brief and apparently trifling illness, in his fifty-third year. His loss at this time was a great one. A gentleman of good administrative ability, and of fine scholarship, a thorough educator, no one, perhaps, had mastered the detailed interests of Dickinson College more fully. He had adhered to the College with pertinacity of purpose and unwavering faith in its ultimate success during the darkest hours of its history, and it seemed a sad Providence that prevented the enjoyment of the more favorable conditions for its advancement just assured. In all intercourse with him, as student and colleague, the writer had found him a thorough, uniform gentleman. The College was administered by Professor Hillman, the senior professor, as acting President, until the election of Rev. Robert L. Dashiell, D. D., of the class of 1846, in September of the same year. The latter resigned the position at the end of four years, to enter upon his duties as Missionary Secretary, to which position he had been elected by the General Conference of the Church, as the successor of Dr. Durbin. At the ensuing meeting of the trustees, the present incumbent, Rev. James A. McCauley, D. D., of the class of 1847, was elected president.

Chapter VII.

BOARD OF TRUSTEES.

Original Constitution—Clerical Representation—
Principal ex-officio President—Vacation of Seats—
Change in Tenure of Office.

HE success of a college depends to so great a degree upon the body from which emanate all measures connected with it, and in which the decision of all matters concerning its interests is finally lodged, that the manner in which it is constituted and perpetuated is of the highest interest. In these particulars institutions differ very widely, and most of them have, at times, experienced changes, with some real or fancied advantage in view. The original charter of Dickinson College placed it "under the management, direction, and government of a number of trustees, not exceeding forty, or a quorum or board thereof." This quorum, in a subsequent section, was fixed at nine members, but to dispose of property, required the assent of at least seven. The forty individuals named as trustees in the act of incorporation, and their successors, were empowered to fill vacancies, as they might occur, by new elections, and thus perpetuate the body, with the restriction that the number of clergymen, one third of the number, should not be diminished, and that neither the principal nor professors, whilst they remain such, should be capable of the office of trustee. In 1826, the first restriction was altered so as to prevent more than one third, at any time, from being clergymen, and in 1834, the

principal was made *ex-officio* president of the board of trustees,
with all the rights of any other member ; at the same time the
discipline of the College was vested in the faculty, they being
held responsible for the proper exercise of it, and an omission
in the original charter, of any provision for the removal of
trustees who neglected the duties of the office, was remedied,
by giving the board power to declare the seats of members vacant who shall have been absent from the meetings of the
board for two years, or who shall, from any cause, be rendered
incapable for one year, of attending to the duties of the office.

Within the past ten years, many suggestions have been made
of modifications in the mode of election, and in the tenure of
office of members of the board, looking mainly to a more intimate organic connection of the patronizing Conferences and
of the Alumni with the Institution.   As a result, the Board,
with great cordiality, extended an invitation to the official visitors, appointed from year to year, from the Conferences, and
five visitors, appointed by the Alumni Association, to be present
at its sessions and to deliberate with it, and directed that said
visitors be notified of the resolution and times of meeting.
Notices are accordingly sent, as to members of the Board, and
visitors have generally been in attendance, and taken part in the
discussions.   Those from the Alumni Association are elected
by that body for five years, the term of one visitor expiring
each year.   A complete revision of the charter was made at
the sessions of 1878 and 1879.   The subject of Alumni representation in the Board was fully considered and strongly advocated by some, but it seemed to be the judgment of the majority that it was not expedient, especially in view of the fact
that the Board, at present, is largely constituted of Alumni.
Certainly, the College is largely indebted for valuable counsel,
as well as substantial aid, to many who are not Alumni.   The
most marked change, however, which is to go into effect at the

meeting in 1879, is the limitation of the tenure of office of members of the Board to four years, and the election of one fourth of the Board every year. There seems to have been, practically, no dissent on the part of members of the Board of Trustees, or of the Conferences, to this change, whilst, by many, it is regarded as full of promise for increased vigor and interest in the administration of the College.

Chapter VIII.

FINANCES.

College Finances in General—State Aid to Dickinson —Endowment in 1840—Management of Funds—Loans from Education Boards—Conference Collections— Revenue in 1853—Scholarship Endowment Plan— Western Investments—Last Loan from the Education Boards -- Centenary Endowment — Sunday School Medals—Present Financial Condition—No Debt—At what Sacrifice—Educational Collections Discontinued—Centennial of the College, the Methodist Conference, and the Nation.

HE finances of most literary institutions of higher grade are chronically bad. A financier diagnosing the state of any college at any time during nine tenths of its history, would pronounce its case hopeless. This results from a fundamental difference between institutions organized to make money, and those organized to spend it. Colleges spend all their income, at least, and consequently accumulate no surplus fund to meet inevitable losses by investment or otherwise. The wealth and benevolent disposition of the churches, upon which they generally rest, con-

stitute their reserve fund. The contributions of the Church
are not made to be hoarded, but to be used, not recklessly or
extravagantly, but wisely, and under a full sense of responsibility. A missionary committee that would economize with a
view to a comfortable surplus, would hardly be in accord with
the advanced sentiment of a Church. A college Board of Trustees is a somewhat similar body. From the necessity of the
case, then, colleges are never happy financially, and it requires
very little mismanagement to render their condition desperate.
But founded upon impulses that can always be touched, few,
very few, die from impecuniosity. The incidental allusions to
finances in the preceding pages, show Dickinson to be no exception to the rule. The early records of the Trustees are
taken up with reports of desperate needs, resolutions to raise
money, plans to raise money, appeals of the most urgent character, &c. Much of the same kind of literature might be furnished from the records since its control by the Methodist
Church, and it would be self-delusion in the friends of the College to hope to see the day when it might be otherwise. One
want met, is only the starting point of a new want to be satisfied, just as absolutely essential to the efficiency and character
of the College. A few words and figures, however, may rea-
sonably be expected upon this interesting subject in connection
with the College.

Up to the year 1833, the College had received at different
times sums amounting to about $50,000 from the State. Upon
the assumption of its support by the Methodist Church at that
time, a balance of $3,000 still due from the State, together with
some bank stock, sufficed to pay off all indebtedness, and leave
a surplus to be applied to repairs and the improvement of the
grounds. Out of subscriptions amounting to nearly $50,000
obtained in the Conferences by the agents, one of whom, Reverend E. Jones, subsequently became Bishop, and the centenary

collections of the Church, about $39,000, were realized and funded up to 1840. This amount was far below the expectations of the friends of the College, doubtless owing in great degree to the severe financial distress throughout the country during that period. The management of these funds was committed to separate Corporate Boards created in the cities of Baltimore and Philadelphia, and in New Jersey. These Boards invest the funds, and pay over the interest to the Trustees of the College. Of the above fund, however, about $10,500 were in the form of loans made to the College at different times to aid in the erection of East College and South College, and for the purchase of books and apparatus. These loans were justified on the ground that the room-rent from the new buildings would more than equal the interest on the loans. To meet the deficiency in the endowment fund, as first proposed, it was resolved by the Conferences to take up collections for the College, annually, in all the congregations in the patronizing territory to make good the interest, as it were. In 1853, $7,000 of this small fund was appropriated to Wesleyan Female College, at Wilmington, by the Philadelphia Conference, on the ground that it had been originally especially contributed for the purposes of female education. The income from all these funds, after this date, amounted to about $1,000 per annum, to which was added receipts from tuition and from the Conference collections before alluded to, which were variable in amount.

In 1851, a plan of endowment, by the sale of cheap scholarships, was first considered, and in 1854 it went into operation, after subscriptions for scholarships had reached the minimum of $100,000 as fixed in the plan. The expectation was not only to accumulate a fund in this way sufficient to place the College above pressing wants, but, also, to increase the number of students. Certificates of scholarship, available for four years tuition in the College were sold for $25 ; for ten years, for $50, and for twenty-five years, for $100. The plan was an excellent one, but poorly executed. The minimum was too low, the expenses of working it were too great, and the collection of the notes given for scholarships not closely enough made. The net proceeds did not amount to $60,000, not much more than one third of the amount originally suggested. The most encouraging result, was the increased interest awakened, not simply in the College, but in the subject of higher education among the people, and the number of students rapidly increased. This fund, like the preceding ones, was entrusted to the Education Boards of the Conferences. The floating debt of the College, about the same time, was $4,000, in part remaining from the erection of East College, and in part accumulated deficiencies, and to this was added a deficiency by the falling off in tuition before interest could be realized from the receipts for the endowment scholarships. This was met for greater part by new loans from the Education Boards of the Conferences; the Baltimore Conference, however, replaced almost the entire amount thus loaned by it by special collections.

In 1856, in order to increase the revenue, $42,000 of the funds were invested in Galena and Milwaukee at twelve per cent. upon real estate security. Interest was paid punctually for a few years, when it began to come in tardily from some investments, and in other cases, it became necessary to foreclose the mortgages and purchase the properties. As current expenses could not be met by accumulated interest, however secure it might be, financial distress soon became very great, and further loans amounting to $10,997 were made by the Education Boards to discharge the floating debts, and a mortgage was given by the Trustees of the College to those corporations for the full amount of all loans made to the College up to that time. Such relief, of course, could only be of the most temporary character, especially when for a year no interest was received from the Baltimore fund. In 1866, a similar crisis in affairs occurred, by reason of an accumulated floating debt without sufficient revenue from ordinary sources to hope to liquidate it, and continue the operations of the College on as broad a basis. It was again agreed to ask a loan from the Education Boards, with the distinct understanding that no further accommodation of the character would be asked, and that the College should be presented as a prominent object for the Centenary offerings of the Church in that year. From these efforts, the sum of $100,000 was realized, and what was of almost as great importance to the College, greater interest in it was again awakened. The donations for the most part were small in amount. The Sunday Schools contributed a large amount ; each child contributing one dollar being entitled to a medal with the impress of the College and its motto on one side. These funds, like the preceding, were entrusted almost exclusively to the Education Boards. Since then, the current income has been sufficient for ordinary current expenses, and to permit at times necessary repairs.

Although the recent financial crisis has affected some of the investments, they have been in the main of such a character as to continue productive, and some that have been regarded as almost valueless for years, have appreciated, so as to more than repair losses previously experienced. Thus property in Milwaukee has become salable, and what remains undisposed of, though unproductive at present, has a market value of $10,000. A bequest of Thomas Kelso, late of Baltimore, of $10,000, is payable in 1880, and a bequest of $1,000 of Dr. John Fisher, also late of Baltimore, has been received during the past year. The endowment fund at present amounts to $208,000, of which about $52,000 is unproductive. The latter, including besides the Milwaukee property, worth $10,000,

6

and the Kelso bequest of $10,000, the loans made to the College by the Education Boards amounting to more than $31,000.

The financial administration of the College during the past twelve years can be characterized as eminently conservative. The College is, in consequence, at present in a condition to present its claims upon the Church for recognition, with the assurance that every dollar contributed will go directly toward increasing the efficiency of the institution, and not be required to discharge accumulated indebtedness. At the same time this strong financial position has unquestionably been retained at the sacrifice of numbers, and the prestige that new buildings, enlarged courses of study, and other advertising agencies impart. Another loss of influence experienced by the College occurred in the discontinuation of the Conference collections after 1866. Although the financial returns from these were small, and by too great urgency, when in financial distress, they may have made an unfavorable impression in many cases in regard to the College, they served to keep before the people the whole subject of higher education, and its claims upon the benevolence of the Church. There seems to be no doubt that at the concurrence of the interesting centennial celebrations, in 1883, of the establishment of the College, and of the peace that acknowledged the Independence of the Nation, and of that a year later of the organization of the first General Conference of the Methodist Episcopal Church in America, large additions to the resources of the College will be made. The Conferences, as well as the College authorities, have already inaugurated measures with that object in view.

CHAPTER IX

LITERARY SOCIETIES.

THE Belles Lettres and Union Philosophical Societies have always been prominent features of Dickinson College. They date from the very earliest years of the institution, and have been maintained in continuous operation to the present time. As they have always been secret societies, their internal history is shrouded in mystery, but their external manifestations leave no doubt as to their utility in the development of intellectual and true manly character. Scarcely had the the students begun to come together at the new College, before a number of them, under the American instinct of organization, founded the Belles Lettres Society in 1786, on the 22d of February, and on the 31st of August, three years later, the Union Philosophical Society was also organized for "mutual improvement in science and literature." The meetings do not seem to have been held at any regular place until 1791, when the use of Dr. Davidson's lecture-room was granted by the Trustees to the societies on alternate Saturdays. The Belles Lettres desiring to "transact business without interruption," in 1800 met in the old court-house, and continued to do so until the grant of the hall in West College, by the Trustees, in 1808.

In 1791 the nucleus of a library was formed by the Belles Lettres Society, the catalogue of which, however, in 1810, had not outgrown a sheet of paper posted on the door of the hall. Its rival was not long in taking similar measures for the benefit of its members. These libraries, by donations and purchases, have increased, until, combined, they number nearly twenty-one thousand volumes, many of them of great value. They are open twice a week, under common regulations of the Societies, to members of both.

The decided influence of these organizations at an early day has already been alluded to in Chief Justice Taney's account of his college days. Their public exhibitions and debates have always been matters of highest college interest, and although in later years the society feeling has not been so demonstrative, they have continued their public exercises without intermission, and each year, at the usual time, have greeted their friends at their literary festivals.   In the last few years there seems to have been something of a revival of the old interest.   The alumnus of twenty-five years ago would, however, be somewhat disappointed in his successors. He would recall, perhaps, the earnest but generous rivalry, the warm electioneering at the opening of the term, the happy time for the first six weeks of the novitiate in college life, so free from care, so burdened by friends, so shadowed by the few who had him in charge, and how earnest life was allowed to become to him, how wide a circle of acquaintances he was permitted to make after the solemn initiation was over.   He would look in vain for the long processions with their display of the red roses of the Belles Lettres, and the white wreaths of the Unions, displaced by the tasteful but less conspicuous gold badges. He would fail to recognize the brotherly ties of the olden time between members of the same society, hardly less earnest than those of fraternity to-day, with immeasureably more of dignity, and less of the intimacy that frequently demands disagreeable and, perhaps, ungenerous, or even improper concessions.

Even the gold badges of Society, represented in the accompanying cuts, which were first introduced about 1852, and the

wearing of which seemed, at one time, as obligatory on members as that of the roses they had displaced, are now rarely seen. Every member, at the time of their adoption, felt it his duty to submit his taste, judgment, and conscience to the infallibility of his Society on all points, and defend the beauty of the emblem of his Society, especially against all unfavorable comparisons with that of its rival. About 1855, the Belles Lettres, however, officially admitted the ugliness of their policeman's star, a combination of a Maltese cross, laurel wreath, jagged points, and a central topaz, by adopting the present far more classical and beautiful design, the façade of a Grecian temple, with its accompanying motto.

Various causes are assigned for these changes in regard to societies, and doubtless, many are operative. Fraternities may have had something to do with them, but they are not alone. Processions of all kinds went out when the extravagant floral displays on public occasions came in. Faculties and Trustees combined have not been able to hold the students in line. The number and appreciation of his lady friends is a matter of highest importance to the possible future orator, and no undergraduate is without some aspirations in that direction. The removal of the anniversary exhibitions, from commencement week to the middle of the year, has also, undoubtedly, had as great an influence in imparting a peculiar character to these occasions, by rendering them affairs of almost purely local interest. But whilst the old Alumnus might find much to lament,

he might, on closer study, find that in many respects advances and improvements have been made. Perhaps one of the most notable is the institution of prizes in oratory for their members in the Sophomore class, inevitably to be followed by the Freshman burlesque. He would still recognize, too, in all their public exercises, evidences of the same peculiar culture that they have always been credited with.

CHAPTER X.

PREPARATORY SCHOOL.

ESTABLISHED, 1783 — RE-ORGANIZED, 1833 — REASONS FOR ABANDONMENT IN 1869—LOSS OF STUDENTS AND SCHOLARSHIP—ADVANTAGE OF SCHOOL TO STUDENTS AND COLLEGE—RE-ESTABLISHED, 1877—EMORY HALL—SUCCESS.

T the establishment of the College, the advantages of a Preparatory School, in connection with it and under the more immediate care of the faculty, were recognized, and the organization of such a school was the first work of the Trustees. Throughout the first half century of the College, the school continued in existence, and its prosperity was as earnestly considered as that of the College itself. In 1833, the first act of the re-organized Board of Trustees, under the Methodist Church, was the opening of a Preparatory School, and it formed a prominent feature of the re-organized institution, and contributed largely to its prosperity in numbers, and, perhaps, even more to thoroughness in scholarship. Men of first class ability were put in charge of it. Among them occur the names of Bishops Scott and Bowman, Doctor George R. Crooks, Stephen A.

Roszel, and others of eminence. At one time the experiment was made, of connecting it even more intimately with the College, by making its principal a member of the faculty, with a certain amount of work in the College classes, but it was soon abandoned, as unsatisfactory.

The objectionable feature of the school was that the younger pupils occupied rooms in the college buildings, under the same statutory regulations as the students in the college classes, and no distinction in discipline or restraints imposed, could be made between them. This objection increased with the gradual change in college discipline to less rigidity in form and surveillance in details. In 1869, the school had also become an expense to the College, mainly by the reception of scholarships for tuition, contrary to the original intent. Other schools, of lower than collegiate grades, established by the Church, being, at that time, in successful operation, the Preparatory School was abandoned, with the expectation that these schools might furnish even more than the usual supply of students to repair losses by graduation, &c. The result did not justify the expectation. The numbers entering College were not increased. Many young men, impatient of the restraints of school, and anxious to enter upon the active pursuits of life, and, perhaps, even more averse to a change of school associations already formed, as well as to the renewed expense, preferred to remain content with the lower curriculum, and never found their way to any college. The average preparation of the applicants was also found to be less thorough. Many young men, with entrance to college in view, finding in the seminary course much that was not required for admission to college, preferred to prepare upon the required branches alone, with such opportunities as they were able to command, not always of the best, whilst others applied directly from the high schools of the State, well prepared generally, in every thing but the ancient lan-

guages. The alternative was presented of admitting such applicants, with the expectation that they would make good their
deficiencies by extra work, or of rejecting them, with the advice to go elsewhere for further preparation. Whilst some of
the first class, more mature in mind, with well formed habits
of study, could manage to assume a regular position in the
class by earnest application, they always labored under serious
disadvantages. Few of the latter class were known to return
to renew their applications. Most of both of these classes
would have cheerfully acquiesced in a recommendation of the
Faculty to spend a year in further preparation in a school having some connection with the College, and near at hand, and
the standard of scholarship would thus have been more fully
sustained, as well as the numbers increased.

In such a school, too, both economy in time and money in
preparation for college can be promoted, as well as thoroughness
of preparation. It is unreasonable to expect that seminaries, de-
riving most of their large patronage from those who expect to
be satisfied with a general education, below that of the college,
should adapt their courses of study to the wants of the comparatively few who intend to enter college subsequently. The
result is, that much of the time of the student must, necessarily, be spent on branches not required for admission to college, but which are more fully treated in a college course, to
the curtailment of that spent upon studies purely preparatory
to admission to college. So impressed were many of the friends
of the College with facts of this nature, that the establishment
of such a school, near enough to the College to be under its direct supervision, was formally recommended by Conference
resolutions of the Church, and the Trustees, in the summer of
1877, authorized the faculty to inaugurate it. The question of
a suitable building seemed providentially solved. The two
congregations of Methodists had agreed to unite as one in

the new Centenary Church, and Emory Chapel, a tasteful edifice, in which the College was already pecuniarily interested,
was relieved of a debt resting on it, by liberal hearted friends
of the College, add presented to the College. The building
is every thing that is necessary for the purpose, and, besides,
contains a large audience room, used for various society exhibitions, commencement exercises, &c., which, by re-seating
with moveable settees, could easily be converted into a hall for
social purposes in connection with commencement occasions.

The School has been in successful operation for two years,
and has already proved of great benefit to the College, and to
the young men who have attended it, whilst by reason of its
exclusive attention to the preparation of students for college, it
has not, in any appreciable degree, come in conflict with the
other seminaries, which are regarded as tributary to the College, and from which students are admitted to the Freshman
Class, upon the certificate of their instructors, without further
examination.

Chapter XI.

SCIENTIFIC DEPARTMENT—1783—1833.

State of Science—Scientific Education—Interest of
Dr. Rush—Views of Dr. Nisbet—Professor Johnston—
Apparatus—Professor Davidson—Professor McCor-
mick—Purchase of Apparatus through Dr. Rush—
Chemistry recognized—Election of Thomas Cooper,
LL. D.—His Character—Protest—Introductory Lec-
ture—Scientific Work—Priestley's Apparatus—Edi-
tor of The Emporium—Other Publications—Resigna-
tion—Reasons for it—Professor Vethake—Professor
Rogers—Messenger of Useful Knowledge.

HE foundation of the College occurred at a time
of intense activity in the scientific as well as in the
political world, and the revolutions in the former
were no less radical than in the latter. A new era
was approaching, to be characterized largely by its remarkable
scientific discoveries, and the speculations and applications flow-
ing from them. Rapidly accumulating facts were demanding
new adjustment of the old theories for their accommodation or
some entirely new generalization to include them, whilst practical applications were working their way at times against popular prejudices or fancied antagonism to public interests. The
discovery of Oxygen by Priestley, in 1774, especially was be-
ginning to make itself felt, and the chaos of chemical facts,
was fast assuming the character of a chemical philosophy. The
wider generalizations of Lavoisier, destined to become the
foundations of Modern Chemistry, were disputing the ground
with the phlogiston hypothesis, and whilst receiving the cordial

assent of many of the younger chemists, many of the older ones, including Priestley, were disputing the new facts, or ingeniously attempting to reconcile the old theory with them, whilst the train of practical consequences was rapidly increasing. Other branches of science felt a similar impulse. Electricity, apparently exhausted under the lead of Franklin, was soon to manifest itself in a less ostentatious but more practical form, and surprise the world with undreamed of contributions. The applications of steam as a motor were being wrought out so perfectly, in principal at least, that all that was left was mainly matter of details in construction. America had been honorably connected with this scientific awakening. She had an interest in three of the most prominent names. The fame of Franklin was all her own, and his reception abroad as the agent of the Colonies was none the less cordial or respectful because of his eminence as a scientific investigator. His portrait, in Paris, made the fortune of the engraver who published it. The teacher, Benjamin Thompson, of Rumford, N. H., second to no philosopher of his age, although expatriated for his loyalty to the Crown, had received his early education and his impulse to scientific studies at Harvard, and remained at least so far American, that when honors thickened on him he chose to be known as Count Rumford, in remembrance of his early American home. As the founder of the Royal Institution of London, a share can also be claimed for him in the fame of Davy, Faraday, and Tyndall. Although Priestley had made most of his important investigations before he came as an exile to America, his later years at Northumberland, Pa., where he had collected about him a library and laboratory, were by no means spent in inactivity, and his contributions to science form part of the scientific literature of America.

But two societies devoted to the promotion of science have survived from that period to the present—the American Phil-

osophical Society in Philadelphia, the oldest of all, founded by
Franklin, in 1743, and the American Academy of Arts and
Sciences of Boston, founded in 1780.

Scientific instruction in the colleges was provided for by lectures. The chairs of Mathematics and Natural Philosophy were
generally combined, as at Yale, Dartmouth, Princeton, &c.,
but Chemistry was pushing its claims to a more distinct recognition. The labors of Black, Cavendish, Scheele, Lavoisier,
and others, were fast preparing the way for the separation of
this branch from the parent stem of physical science, and as
early as 1774, William and Mary College, Virginia, had a Professor of Chemistry and Natural Philosophy, a chemistry necessarily widely different from that of to-day. The University
of Pennsylvania also had a chair of Natural Philosophy and
Chemistry as early as 1779. The advance of science is well
indicated by the tendency to differentiation of these chairs, and
the establishment of a separate chair for the growing science of
Chemistry, though in many cases, the separation was not permanent. The medical colleges, of which there were but two,
one in New York and the other in Philadelphia, generally combined Materia Medica and Chemistry, and the first chair of
Chemistry in America, was that filled by Dr. Benjamin Rush in
the medical department of the University of Pennsylvania in
1769. He had enjoyed the instruction of Black at Edinburg,
and was doubtless thoroughly master of what there was of a
science of Chemistry at that time, though holding it subordinate
to his medical studies, he has left no special record in it.

The young College was fortunate in having the interest and
counsel of one so liberally cultured in science, and with all so
enthusiastic and public spirited. In his ideal of a college, the
experimental sciences formed a prominent feature as a factor in
a liberal education. In the plans for soliciting funds, which
were very frequently of his devising, philosophical apparatus

was prominently mentioned as one of the needs of the college. In the letter to Honorable Mr. Bingham, requesting him to secure aid abroad, it was included. In urging the acceptance of the principalship upon Dr. Nisbet, he took pains to explain the absence of philosophical apparatus.

From his personal acquaintance with Dr. Nisbet, he had, doubtless, reason to know his appreciation of, and acquaintance with the Physical Sciences. It would have been singular if a man of his intense intellectual activity and decided passion for all kinds of learning, should not have been fully acquainted with the range of scientific thought of that day, especially educated, as he was, under the influences of the University of Edinburgh, where science always had met with more decided recognition than in the universities of England. An account of a conversation, during one of his visits to Governor Dickinson, at Wilmington, upon the probable effect of a zealous and ardent prosecution of the study of the physical sciences on the religious character, indicates to some degree his familiarity with this subject. The conversation occupied the entire evening, Dr. Nisbet taking the lead, by common consent, and maintaining the position that "unless the grace of God produced a different effect, the more intimately men became acquainted with the works of nature, the less mindful were they of their great author." A gentleman present represented it "as one of the most rich, instructive, and interesting intellectual feasts that he ever enjoyed," and at the close, Governor Dickinson remarked, "Doctor, what you have said, would form an invaluable octavo volume. I would give a large sum to have it in that form." It is permitted, therefore, to infer, that as President of the College, he was fully capable of appreciating the earnest efforts of Dr. Rush to increase the efficiency of instruction in these sciences.

As early as 1784, a committee was appointed, including Dr.

Rush, to engage some one to teach Mathematics and Natural Philosophy, and in 1786, Robert Johnston, who had previously acted as tutor in Mathematics, was elected Professor, and at the same time temporarily appointed tutor in Natural Philosophy, with an addition to his salary, for services as the latter. In the same year, the purchase of suitable philosophical apparatus was urged by Doctor Rush, and purchase was made, through him, of the nucleus of the collection, and for " his attention to the interests of the institution," in this matter, the thanks of the Board were voted him. Among the pieces were an electrical-machine, barometer, thermometer, and others not enumerated in detail, but more valuable in the aggregate. Not long after his appointment, in 1787, the trustees, by resolution, attended one of the lectures by Professor Johnston, and upon re-assembling, they resolved that his temporary appointment as tutor of Natural Philosophy should cease, " as it had not answered their wishes or expectations; " and, at the same time, they requested the principal and Professor Davidson, especially the latter, to " give as much attention as possible in instructing and qualifying the class in Natural Philosophy, with a view to graduation at their next meeting." On conference with the principal and Doctor Davidson, it was found that the class could not be prepared by the date fixed, and the examination was accordingly postponed to a more convenient season for the students, according to the system of that day, of graduating students as they became ready, which might not be altogether objectionable, in all cases. Owing to the reduction of salary, occasioned by the loss of the tutorship, Professor Johnston resigned his professorship of Mathematics. Instruction in Natural Philosophy continued to be given by Doctor Davidson, until 1792. He was a man of elegant tastes and accomplishments, with decided acquirements in the direction of physical sciences, and great aptitude in imparting instruc-

tion.   He published some papers on astronomy, which was his
favorite study, and constructed a very ingenious piece of apparatus, called a cosmosphere, by means of which many celestial
problems could be solved.   It was in existence a few years ago,
and was left by will to his son, Reverend Robert Davidson, D.
D., who failed to get it, however, through some mistake of the
executors of the will, who sent him an old microscope instead,
whilst the cosmosphere was sold with the miscellaneous effects.
Apparatus of this character had much more prominence in a
collection then than at present, and some of the most eminent
men, among them Rittenhouse, devoted considerable time to
their production.   Instruction was also given by Doctor Davidson, by special direction of the Board, in Geography and
the use of globes, upon which great stress was laid at that time,
and one of the curiosities left by him, and quite popular at the
time, was an epitome of geography in verse, published during
his connection with the Univerity of Pennsylvania.   As a re-
creation from severer studies, he composed sacred music as well
as verses, and employed his pen so skillfully, that some of his
pen-sketches could scarcely be distinguished from engravings
by experts.   Among his papers, left by him, were many care-,
fully prepared lectures on scientific subjects.   Instruction in
Mathematics and Natural Philosophy seems to have been combined under the Professor McCormick, after 1792, and the
efforts of the instructor seem to have been supplemented by as
generous an outlay for appliances as the College could command.   At one of. the periods of deepest financial embarrassment, in 1797, the Board resolved that, notwithstanding the
insufficiency of the funds, it conceived it highly expedient to
make provision for the improvement of the Philosophical Apparatus, by an annual appropriation for the purpose.   In September, 1805, the committee charged with superintending the
removal of the library and apparatus to the new building, were

authorized to appropriate $200 for maps and additions to the apparatus, as soon as the funds would admit. This was rescinded, after the grant by the State, in 1806, and the first sum of $500, out of that grant, was appropriated for the purpose, and subsequently the amount was increased by $1,000, for apparatus and books, and Doctor Rush was placed upon the committee, by reason of his scientific character and his residence in Philadelphia, the scientific center of the country, as well as on account of his willingness, on all occasions, to give his time to furthering the interests of the College. The selection and purchase of the apparatus were mainly made by him. As apparatus of the kind was generally imported at that time, considerable time was expended in correspondence, and other inevitable delays were encountered. From the reports made of his success and prospects, from time to time, to Carlisle, the principal purchases can be ascertained, and also something of the enthusiasm with which he entered into the matter, as well as the difficulties encountered. Thus, in 1808, he writes: "I have purchased an Electrical and Galvanic Apparatus for $250. The former is the most complete and splendid thing of the kind ever imported into our country. It will add much to the reputation of our College. It will be sent with the Galvanic Apparatus and a small Chemical Apparatus, for showing the composition of air and water, which I have since purchased, by the first wagon, with a careful driver, that offers for Carlisle." After negotiating for an air-pump, first in Boston, afterward in Salem, Massachusetts, and assuring that they would be more complete than those made in Great Britain, he announced that he had "happily succeeded in purchasing a complete and elegant air-pump, from a private gentleman," and expressed himself as obliged for the hint "to offer more to a wagoner to take it, and the other boxes," than was commonly given, the rate finally agreed upon being about ten dollars per hundred.

The gentleman alluded to, from whom the air-pump, a double-barreled one, of excellent construction, was purchased, was John Redman Coxe, of Philadelphia. Among the other purchases were a Hydro-pneumatic Blowpipe, and a Condensing Apparatus, and among the books Chaptal's, Henry's, and Accum's Chemistries, the Chemical Catechism, and Conversations on Chemistry.

With the election of a permanent Principal in 1809, measures were inaugurated for more thorough instruction in the physical sciences. In 1810, it was resolved to establish a chair of Natural Philosophy and Chemistry—the first recognition of the science of Chemistry—and Dr. Frederick Aigster was elected tutor in those branches. At the same time, it was directed, that $250, out of an appropriation of $1,250 recently made for the purchase of apparatus, should be expended for chemical apparatus under the direction of Dr. Aigster and Dr. Davidson, with a request to Dr. Rush that he would attend to the importation of it. Whatever expectations may have been formed from this appointment, which was made very deliberately, and after considerable negotiation, during which Dr. Aigster visited the College at the expense of the corporation, they do not seem to have been realized, as before the close of the year the position became vacant.

The resignation of Dr. Aigster just at this juncture, brought to the College the services of Dr. Thomas Cooper, one of the most remarkable products of the complexity of moral and intellectual forces of the closing quarter of the last century. Generally recognized as a man of the most varied learning and ability, a voluminous and forcible writer upon a great variety of subjects, an able presiding judge for eight years, until impeached and removed in times of high political excitement, he had also proved himself a skillful scientific investigator. But whilst his election undoubtedly imparted unusual interest and

7

vigor to this department of the College, it also thrust it into a kind of prominence that many of its friends regarded as injurious to its best interests. A native of England, educated at Oxford, on terms of intimacy with Pitt, Burke, and other leading English statesmen, a resident of Paris during four months of the Reign of Terror, and enjoying the excitement to the full, he was a radical in politics and a materialist in creed. The friend of Priestley, he shared with the latter his exile from his country, and enjoyed the use of his library and laboratory at Northumberland. In America he met with ready and full appreciation by the radical school of politicians, and had their sympathy under what were regarded by them as religious persecutions. For many years he enjoyed the friendship of Jefferson and Madison. As a judge, his ability was of a high order. His opinion on the effect of a sentence of a foreign admiralty court was widely circulated, and was regarded by Madison as irrefragible disproof of the British doctrine. Among his other legal works, was a revised translation of the Institutes of Justinian, with references to parallel passages in the Civil Law, the Law of England, and American Reporters.

The vacant professorship had been referred to the Committee of Visitors of the Board of Trustees, with authority to employ some suitable person to fill it for one year. At a meeting of the board a month later, this Committee submitted a correspondence had with Thomas Cooper, Esq. A motion to enter into an election of a Professor of Chemistry and Mineralogy was only carried after decided opposition, and at a subsequent meeting, a written protest was entered upon the minutes on the part of the absent members, alleging that the previous meeting was irregular, and expressing a belief that the "election of Mr. Cooper would prove highly injurious to the interest and reputation of the College, in consequence of the prejudices entertained by the public against him." At the urgent solicitation

of the board, at considerable inconvenience, he entered upon
the position a few months earlier than he had intended, and
two days after taking the oath of office, August 7, 1811, his
Introductory Lecture on Chemistry was delivered in the " public
hall " of the College, attended by the Board of Trustees as a
body, as well as by the students.   It was published by order of
the Board, and is remarkable for its exhaustiveness and as being
one of the very earliest scientific lectures published in the country.   The lecture itself filled one hundred pages octavo, and
the accompanying notes added one hundred and thirty-six more
pages, displaying a wonderful range of information.   After
general observations on man's relations to his environment, and
a general classification of scientific knowledge, reasons were
assigned for anticipating a course of lectures on Chemistry by
a history of that science, contrary to the general opinion that
it would more profitably follow such a course, accompanied by
the statement that he knew of no tolerable history of Chemistry in the English language.   The Scriptures were first searched
for chemical facts, because they carry " marks of internal evi-
dence that entitle them to great consideration."   Then passing
in review the Chemistry of the Egyptians, Greeks, Romans,
Hindoos, Chinese, and that of the dark ages, he considered the
more scientific phase of the phlogiston period enriched by the
labors and ingenuity of Boyle, Stahl, Black, Cavendish, and
the discovery of Oxygen by Priestley.   Unqualified assent was
given to the new theory, and an extravagant opinion of Lavoisier as a scientific man was expressed.   The " Doctrine of
Heat " and " Galvanic Chemistry " were then discussed as well
as Mineralogy and Geology, followed by a closing statement
of the uses of chemistry.   The notes were particularly full on
mineralogical nomenclature and classification, with a list of
minerals according to Werner's and Hauy's, accompanied by
suggestions of his own as to modifications of the nomenclature.

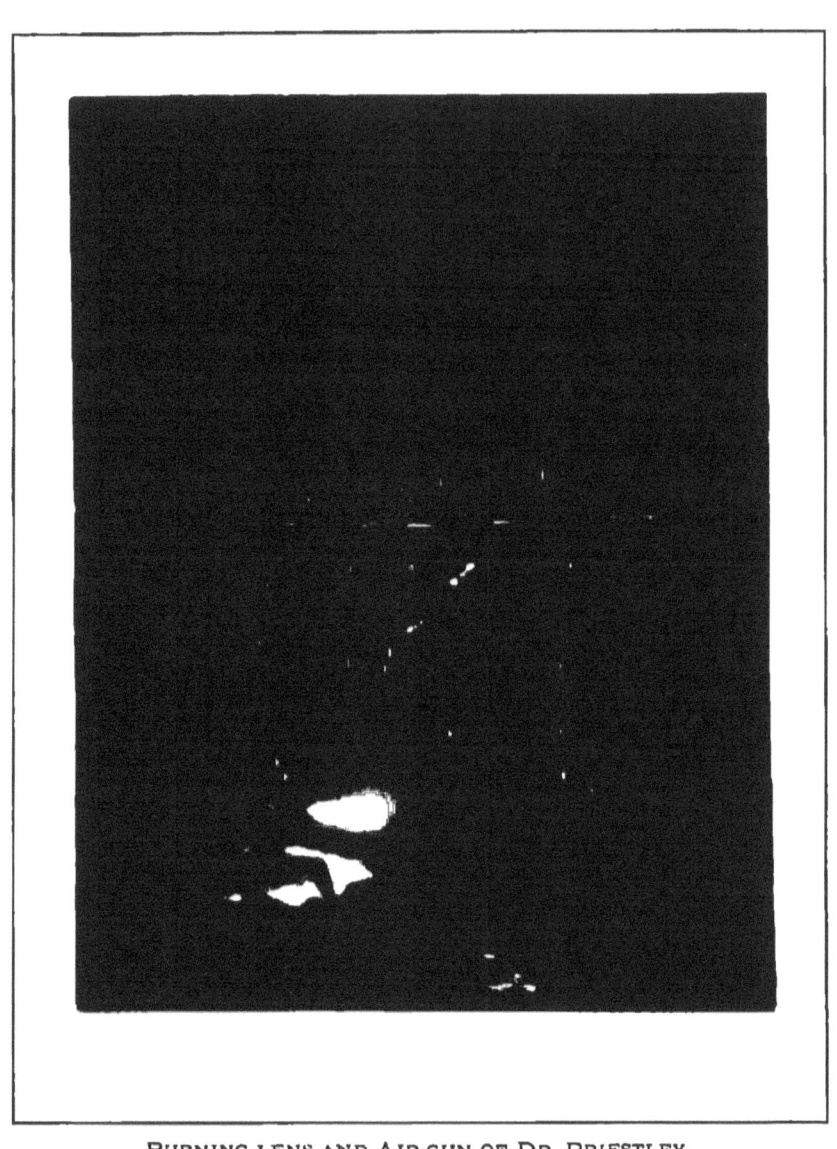

BURNING-LENS AND AIR-GUN OF DR. PRIESTLEY.

ROTASCOPE OF PROFESSOR WALTER R. JOHNSON.

The notes are still more remarkable from the statement that his library was still under the same roof with Dr. Priestley, at Northumberland, and he had been obliged to trust to his memory, but that he had verified every statement that the college library had enabled him to consult.

He seems to have devoted considerable attention to practical chemistry before his arrival in America. Having learned in France the secret of making chlorine from common salt, he made an unsuccessful attempt to apply it, at Manchester, in bleaching and printing calico. In 1811 he published an account, accompanied by a plate of the apparatus employed, of "The decomposition of potash and the production of potassium by heat," which had been accomplished at Priestley's laboratory, at Northumberland, and constitutes the first record of the production of potassium in this country by the furnace process. His repution as a practical chemist attracted students to the College for the study of technical chemistry. The Dupont's, of Delaware, were among his pupils. Although Professor of Chemistry and Mineralogy, he also gave instruction in Natural Philosophy, in connection with Professor M'Cormick. The Seniors and Juniors were required to attend his lectures, and irregular students and others were permitted to attend upon payment of a fee of $10. He was also authorized to employ an assistant in his work, and purchase such "mixtures, drugs, &c.," as he might need. By special authorization of the Board, he purchased the burning-lens, telescope, and air-gun, at present in the college collection, which had been the property of Priestley, the discoverer of oxygen.

In literary labors he was abundant. He revived the Emporium of Arts and Sciences, one of the very earliest journals of a general scientific character published in America, and previously edited by Dr. J. Redman Coxe, of Philadelphia. It appeared bi-monthly, in numbers of one hundred and fifty pages each, at the price of $7 per year. It was continued by Dr. Cooper, on the same plan of "judicious selections of practical papers on the manufactures and the arts from foreign publications, and a repository for original papers of the same description, furnished by men of research in our own country," and assumed in his hands a high scientific character, and was filled with original researches and vigorous criticisms, being profusely illustrated with excellent engravings. Among his minor editorial notices he called attention to the conversion of starch into sugar, just discovered, and describes the molasses produced as "sufficiently similar to the common article, and sweet enough to be used with coffee," and advised the substitution of "evaporated decoction of malt" for the starch, by which the expense of the oil of vitriol, which prevented its use, could be so far reduced as to justify the experiment in every family. The sugar manufacturers seem to have waited nearly three quarters of a century to take the hint. A student in his laboratory contributed a table of colors imparted to "burning cotton dipped in some of the neutral salts in spirit of wine," not only interesting as including the germ of spectroscopic chemistry, but from the manner in which the inevitable sodium continually contributes a trace of yellow to colors otherwise accurately described. The journal ceased in 1814, the long delay of the final volume being explained by "the printers serving their country as volunteers." He also prepared an American edition of Accum's Chemistry, in two volumes, enriched by a copious appendix by himself, in which he manifests a disposition, even at that late date, to champion, to some extent, the phlogiston theory. He remarks: "Facts seem to indicate that there is such a substance as phlogiston, that there is but one body capable of being burned, hydrogen." A peculiar feature of the book is the theories of geology, in separate chapters, of Burnet, Woodward, Whiston, Hutchinson, Moray le

Cot, Maillet, Buffon, Raspé, Worthington, Whitehurst, De Luc, Milne, Hutton, Williams, Delanatherie, Howard, Bertrand, and Kirwan.   In 1818 he also edited an American edition of Thomson's System of Chemistry, in four volumes, and in the same year published a treatise on Medical Jurisprudence.   As his election had taken place under protest, and his religious views were wholly out of accord with those of the majority of the intelligent people from whom patronage was to be expected, there were constant sources of irritation, although in his opening lecture he was more respectful toward prevalent religious opinions than might have been expected. Owing mainly to these causes, his connection with the College terminated, by resignation, September 28, 1815.   He considered himself persecuted for opinion's sake, and had the sympathy of Jefferson and Madison in his misfortunes.   He subsequently became President of South Carolina College, where he remained until 1834.   He died May 1, 1840, at the advanced age of eighty-one years.

The department had been liberally supplied with all necessary appliances during the administration of Professor Cooper, and had a high reputation, but it began to share in the general depression experienced by the College at this time, and no particular provision seems to have been made for it until the reorganization of the College, in 1821, when Henry Vethake, LL. D., was elected Professor of Mathematics and Natural Philosophy, with the duties of the Chair of Chemistry in addition, until suitable provision could be made for it.   His services were secured by remarkably liberal remuneration for that time, and large expenditures were made for apparatus and minerals, and for fitting up a laboratory.   In 1826 John Vethake, M. D., was appointed Lecturer on Chemistry for a year.   In 1827 John K. Finley, M. D., was engaged to deliver a winter course of lectures on chemistry, and the Senior class in the German Reformed Theological Seminary was allowed to attend the lectures. In the following year he was elected Professor of Chemistry and Natural Philosophy, and in 1830 was succeeded by Henry D. Rogers, A. M., who afterward became the eminent geologist of Pennsylvania, whose history, with that of his brother, Professor William B. Rogers, forms so large and creditable a part of the scientific history of the country. Whilst connected with the College he edited "The Messenger of Useful Knowledge," a monthly magazine of scientific character, and also containing essays on educational, literary, agricultural, and political subjects, and valuable information from foreign journals. Upon the latter feature was based one expectation of patronage. One number contained an article on Dew, by Professor William B. Rogers, then Professor in William and Mary College. In a review of the state of the scientific world, the nature of light and heat is spoken of as "the key to physical science yet to be discovered, when the door will be thrown open, and a new and attractive field presented to view, in which simplicity, harmony, and beauty, will be found to pervade the material universe." With his resignation, in 1830, the magazine also ceased. The radical defects in the organic law of the College rendered positions in it very unattractive.

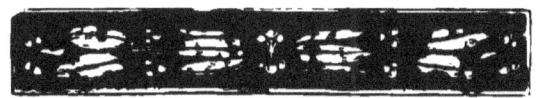

Chapter XII.

SCIENTIFIC DEPARTMENT, 1833 TO 1865.

Interest of Dr. Durbin in Science—Professor Allen — Apparatus — Professor Baird — Scientific Excursions—Cave Exploration—Called to the Smithsonian — Secretary of the Latter — Services to Science and Literary work—Professor Wentworth —Missionary—Editor—Professor Wilson—Difficulties of the Position—Success and Characteristics as a Teacher—His Death.

AT the re-organization of the College, under the control of the Methodist Church, the Department of Natural Science was fortunate in the selection of Dr. Durbin as the organizing head of the College. His full sympathy with all branches of human learning, accompanied by such a familiarity with physical science as had led to his election to the professorship of Natural Science in Wesleyan University, was reinforced by an intense appreciation of the natural world and its varied phenomena. His exquisite description of Chamounix, unsurpassed in all the literature of travel since, alone would be sufficient to establish this feature of his character. The professorship of Natural Science was one of the earliest-filled in the re-organized Faculty, in 1834, and measures were at once taken for increasing the collection of apparatus; and whilst endeavoring to accumulate the endowment fund first proposed, and soliciting funds or even obtaining them by loan for

the erection of East College, he could not resist the temptation
to acquire what was at that time a fine collection of apparatus,
belonging to Professor Walter R. Johnson, of Philadelphia,
which had been employed by him as Secretary of the Franklin
Institute. He was about to assume a position in the Wilkes'
Exploring Expedition, which, for some reason, he finally failed
to accept, and was thus left without apparatus. Among the
pieces was the Rotascope, employed by him in his investigations of Rotary Motion,* and which was noticed as anticipating
some of the peculiarities of the Gyrascope, in 1856.† The
collection was secured for $2,000, although its original cost
had been $5,000. It was necessary for Dr. Durbin to assume
the responsibility of the purchase, and he unhesitatingly did
so, supported by four gentlemen of Philadelphia, and in spite
of the hard times, collected one half of the money during the
course of the year. In a letter to the writer, a few years before
his death, he alluded to it as the "magnificent apparatus," and
adds, "but progress has left my once cherished *basis* of philosophical apparatus far behind." Its transportation from Philadelphia was no small matter at that day, and was superintended
by Professor Allen, who then filled the chair of Natural Science.
It was transhipped on wagons at Columbia, Pa., and reached
Carlisle with but one article damaged. During Dr. Durbin's
visit to the East the interests of the College seem to have been
continually present to him. At the Giant's Causeway he secured
three large sections of columns, of three pieces each, besides a
complete wooden model; at Chamounix he procured a model of
the valley and Mount Blanc chain; in Egypt he secured several
mummies of the Sacred Ibis, together with other minor specimens. It is but natural to assume that he was not so much in

---

* Am. Jour. Sci., Vol. XXI, 1st Ser., (1832) p. 265.
† Am. Jour. Sci., Vol. XXI, 2d Ser., p. 146.

earnest in regard to these appliances as static elements of mere
display, but as dynamical elements of instruction, and that he
would be equally solicitous in regard to the instructor.   In 1834
Col. Thomas E. Sudler, of St. Johns College, was elected Professor of Natural Science, and upon his declination in the spring
of the year following, the College was fortunate in securing
the services of William H. Allen, A. M.   A graduate of Bowdoin College, he had been engaged in teaching Latin and Greek
for two years, and at the time of his election had charge of the
High School at Augusta, Me.   Elected as Lecturer on Natural
Science for the first year, at the close of that engagement he
was elected professor.   Under his administration for twelve
years the department enjoyed a great measure of popularity.
He was a gentleman of decided ability in different departments
of study, and of consummate tact in administration.   As a
teacher he impressed the students with a belief in his infallibility on questions of science, and as a lecturer he was clear and
full, and possessed the happy faculty of seizing the salient points
of his subject and keeping them in view until fixed in the memory.   The apparatus was enlarged, and loans were even authorized at times for the purpose.   The branches of Electricity and
General Chemistry were, perhaps, best represented, and an inventory made at the time shows a number of pieces, effective
then, which, by the rapid advance of science, have been rele-
gated to historic niches, whilst their modern successors hardly
exhibit traces of relationship, and the whole mode of instruction has been made to yield to the strain of the same advance.

Upon the election of Professor Allen to the chair of English
Literature and Philosophy, in 1848, Spencer F. Baird, was
elected to the chair of Natural Science.   A native of Reading, Pa., he had received his education in the College, entering
the preparatory department in 1835, and graduating, at the age
of seventeen, in the class of 1840.   He had been connected with

the College since 1845, as Curator of the Museum and Professor of Natural History, and the College had had the advantage, not only of his services, but of his large collection of specimens in Natural History, perhaps unequaled, in some of its classes, in the country.   His enthusiastic and unreserved devotion to science was calculated to awaken a deep interest in its study in the College, and a number of young men, who afterward achieved eminence, received their impulse from him.   He was a gentleman of great ability for organization and administration, as well as of broad scientific culture, traits that have contributed so largely to his usefulness in his subsequent connection with the Smithsonian Institution, at Washington.   He continued his devotion to his specialty of Natural History, more particularly Ornithology, although he also published a descriptive list of the surrounding flora.   He made excursions of many miles on foot, throughout the State of Pennsylvania, in pursuit of facts and specimens connected with his favorite studies.   In one of his tramps, in the neighborhood of Carlisle, it is said that whilst hammering away at a rock, in search of fossils, he was on the point of being arrested as an escaped lunatic.   But the rustic council of war did not furnish any one courageous enough to make the arrest.   During his connection with the College he also explored the cave on the Conedoguinet, a point of considerable local interest, with numberless traditions clustering around it.   He extracted much of scientific interest from it.   At that day cave-hunting had not assumed the character of a distinct and intensely interesting branch of scientific investigation, as at present.   Large quantities—wagon-loads—of organic remains were removed, including bones of all the species of mammals found in Pennsylvania, with the only exceptional feature of excess in size over those of the present day.   A few years ago, the broken thread of these investigations of more than a quarter of a century before, was resumed by him, and a more exhaustive examination exhibited the usual kitchen-midden characteristics. The resignation of Professor Baird, in 1850, was occasioned by the superior advantages for the prosecution of the branches of science to which he had especially devoted himself, offered him as Assistant Secretary of the Smithsonian Institution, with especial charge of the National Museum, a position he filled with such eminent ability that, by common consent, he was recognized as the most fitting successor to Professor Henry, as Secretary, upon the death of the latter, in 1878. His departure was a matter of great regret to all connected with the College, and he was, at the same time, elected to fill a vacancy in the Board of Trustees, and continued to act with that body, until pressure of other duties began to interfere with his regular attendance.

The services of Professor Baird to science, in connection with the Smithsonian, cannot be overestimated. Among his labors, in addition to those of his office, he has, for a number of years, as United States Commissioner of Fisheries, done much to encourage pisciculture, by investigating the habits of food fishes, and stocking the streams of the country with varieties of fish suitable to them. During the sessions of the Commission of Halifax, his services were in constant requirement. He has also utilized the vast resources of the Smithsonian files of all the scientific journals of the world, in editing the invaluable Annual Record of Science and Industry, published from year to year, by Harper & Brothers, and has made the Scientific Record, in the Monthly Magazine of those publishers, worthy of the established character of that publication.

The election of a suitable successor to Professor Baird was no easy matter. As has been elsewhere mentioned, Reverend Erastus Wentworth, D. D., a highly esteemed minister of the Methodist Church, and, at the time, President of McKendree

College, Illinois, was unanimously chosen. Educated at Caze-
novia Seminary and Wesleyan University, he had, immediately
after graduation, taught Natural Science in the academy at
Governeur, New York, and afterward in that at Poultney, Ver-
mont. His connection, for four years, with McKendree College, had been highly creditable to him. As a professor in
Dickinson, he was a popular instructor, and fully met the expectations entertained at his election, although better known as
a preacher, and as a graceful and vigorous writer. Although
the department moved on largely under the impulse it had received, and was not enlarged or made particularly prominent
under his administration of it, the course was, doubtless, as full
and as efficiently carried out, as in most of the colleges at that
time. In 1854, he was called from the College by the Church
to engage in missionary work at Foo Chow, China, in which
field he labored, with marked success, for a number of years.
He also afterward, at the call of the Church, edited the *Ladies'
Repository*, with marked ability. In proceeding to fill the vacant chair, the trustees first resolved to appoint a Lecturer on
Natural Science, with the duties of a professor, and William
C. Wilson was elected to that position, for one year. A native
of Elkdale, Chester county, Pennsylvania, a graduate of the
class of 1850, with distinction, he had been successfully engaged in teaching in a classical school, in Chester county, Pennsylvania. He was a comparatively young man, of broad culture, vigorous intellect, and enthusiastic disposition, and of
tastes and aptitudes in the direction of the exact and experimental sciences, and withal, a layman, and, consequently, perfectly free to devote himself exclusively to the prosecution of
his favorite studies. The selection was one full of promise to
the College.

The entrance upon such a position is necessarily attended
with embarrassments and labors from which other departments

are free. To take an inventory of the educational appliances in the way of apparatus, may be the work of a few days, but to learn its condition and availability for instruction, involves most patient, careful, and time-consuming investigation, and testing frequently only to reveal that it is defective or perhaps worthless, or requires much more expenditure of time and labor for adjustment. Even then some unnoticed apparently trifling peculiarity may remain as a cause of mortifying failure. It was the writers privilege to listen to Professor Wilson's first course of lectures, and, under all the circumstances, they may be described as highly successful. As a lecturer, he was perhaps, by nature, too impulsive, or even impatient, and consequently wanting in that deliberation and delicacy of manipulation often essential to the highest success, but he rapidly improved in these particulars, and as his experiments were always well chosen and adapted to the purpose, he became, with greater familiarity with the apparatus at his disposal, eminently successful as an instructor. Not satisfied with the prosecution of his studies within the limited range of facilities offered by the College, he availed himself, during his vacations, of the advantages of study in the laboratory of the eminent chemist, Dr. F. A. Genth, of Philadelphia, now Professor in the University of Pennsylvania.

The characteristic manifested in his first encounter with his class, of absence of respect for or toleration of cram or sham knowledge, grew with his growth as a teacher, and was but the legitimate outgrowth of a character permeated in every fiber with sterling homesty and conscientiousness. His contributions to the Quarterly Review and occasional addresses, exhibit him as a careful, clear, and vigorous writer. Soon after his election, the department began to sympathize with the college in the distracting influences of the increasing political excitement, and during the war, it suffered with it in its struggle for existence. Some efforts were made to enlarge the course of scientific studies, but as they were made in the direction of post-graduate privileges, they produced no decided or permanent effect. Overwork, exposure in the ill-ventilated rooms occupied as laboratory and office, had much to do in developing a disease, which for years before his death rendered physical labor irksome, and which, finally, resulted fatally. His indomitable will kept him at his post to the last. His last lectures were delivered in his chair. He died March 2, 1865, calmly and without fear, in his thirty-eighth year. What he might have accomplished as a scientific man under more favorable circumstances, it is of course difficult to say, but that he accomplished all that could have been done by any one in his position under the circumstances, is unquestionable. He was eminently social in his disposition and warm in his attachments, and in spite of a manner at times somewhat brusque and abrupt, he is kindly remembered by those who came into intimate contact with him.

Chapter XIII.

SCIENTIFIC DEPARTMENT—ENLARGED COURSE—1866.

General Demand for Increased Attention to Scientific Studies—Obstacles to any Modification of the College Curriculum—Recent Agitation—Opinions of Leading Educators—Elective Studies—Introduction into Dickinson—First Laboratory—Object of the Course and Place of Scientific Studies—Methods of Instruction—Text-Book, Lectures, Practice by the Student—Branches Best Adapted to Practice—Charges for use of Laboratory—Practical Courses Open to Selection—Lectures by the Student—Disciplinary Advantages of Photographic Practice—Scientific Patience.

T the establishment of the College, in 1783, as has already been noticed, the physical sciences occupied, necessarily, a subordinate place, but the rapid increase in the body of scientific facts, the expanding generalizations, above all, the wonderful and varied applications, that came in contact, more or less, with every member of society, together with the grave questions that at some points were thrusting themselves into prominence, all contributed to excite a more general interest in these branches of human knowledge. About the close of the first quarter of this century these influences culminated in an animated discussion of the relation of the colleges to these branches. As the college curriculum seemed fully pre-occupied, the suggestion of new studies was equivalent to that of

crowding others out, or into narrower limits, or of lengthening the time. The latter was not practicable, and as the ancient languages formed so large a part of the course, their curtailment seemed the most feasible plan, the suggestion of which formed, of course, a *casus belli* against the sciences on the part of the advocates of the ancient languages. Against any change were arrayed an established routine, the part the branches assailed had unquestionably played as an educational means through a long past, the sentimental attachment of the body of educated men to the course they had pursued, and the fact that the education it gave was, as Herbert Spencer would term it, the fashionable education of the day, the education of the leading gentlemen of the period. On the other hand, the demands of the advocates of change were vague and uncertain, perhaps extravagant, their plans crude, and there was a well-founded fear as to the extent and radical character the innovations might assume. But in addition to all these adverse influences, the advocates of science confounded to too great a degree useful information and education. It is not surprising, therefore, that some plans of collegiate education, hastily adopted, were soon abandoned, and that the questions at issue seemed experimentally settled, nor more so, that at the revival of the discussion, at a more recent period, this fact should have been used as an argument. Although no permanent direct effect in favor of larger scientific education seemed to result from the agitation that occupied the collegiate world for a number of years, it undoubtedly indirectly stimulated these departments in the colleges into greater activity, and imparted to them greater importance. It was about this time that Dr. Durbin assumed the administration of the college, under the Methodist Episcopal Church, and his thorough comprehension of the educational needs and demands of the day doubtless led him to make the unusually ample provision for scientific

8

instruction, already alluded to, in spite of the financial feebleness of the institution.

But the continued advance of science, and its almost start-
ling applications rapidly succeeding each other, were not calculated to allow the question to remain as *res adjudicata.* After
a comparative quiet of about a quarter of a century the whole
subject seemed to open up anew. The questions assumed sub-
stantially the form : How far can a liberally educated man
afford to be ignorant of the facts and laws of the material universe around him? How far is their study disciplinary? How
far is it possible to recognize tastes, tendencies, and future pursuits in life without sacrificing any essential element of a liberal
education? An exceedingly able and exhaustive report of a
Parliamentary Commission of investigation of some of the leading Great Schools of England, including Eton College, created
quite a sensation, even outside of that country. It embodied
the opinions of leading educators and scientists of Great Britain,
and presented the unexpected fact, that whilst the studies were
almost exclusively classical, the attainments were of a disgrace-
fully low order. One of its conclusions was, that "the best
form of discipline may not be the same in the nineteenth century as it was in the sixteenth, and the information which will
be serviceable in life is sure to be very different."

The criticisms called forth by the ridiculous results, upon the
manner of teaching the classics were perhaps the most valuable
contribution made by this investigation to educational science,
and although they were not applicable to nearly the same extent to American schools, yet here, as there, they opened up
the consideration of the mode of teaching the ancient languages
in a course of liberal education. The question became, not so
much, whether these languages should be abridged to make
room for scientific studies, as, whether they could not be so
taught as to leave room for the latter. With a thorough ap-

preciation of the study of physical science as a disciplinary
agent, John Stuart Mill preferred that the reformers should
point their attacks against the "shameful inefficiency of the
schools that pretended to teach Latin and Greek," with their
"wretched methods of teaching," and with the assurance that
sufficient time would be found for everything else. In this
connection, he suggested as one instance of reform the merely
optional study of metrical rules, as concerning simply the
technicalities of the poet's art, necessary for criticism, but un-
essential for the complete enjoyment of the poetry. According to Mr. Farrar, Greek and Latin, taught in a shorter time
and more comprehensive manner, should form the basis of an
education. So, too, Professor Bowen attributed the decline of
interest in classical study in part to the more minute attention
paid to "the mysteries of Greek accentuation, and the meta-
physics of the subjunctive mood." Another of the ablest and
most accomplished advocates of the classics, Professor Porter,
now President, of Yale, asked whether the importance attached
to grammatical analysis has not seriously interfered with more
important benefits. After the Freshmen year he would let the
lessons be very long, in comparatively easy authors, and the
attention be paid to the import, and would expect the teacher
to "foster an intellectual spirit and an aesthetic feeling for the
peculiarities in thought and diction of the author." This plan
of teaching, it is true, requires not only the conscientious and
enthusiastic teacher, but also a full and experienced one. In
these discussions, many of the leading advocates of scientific
studies readily conceded the value of a certain amount and
character of study of the ancient languages in a liberal education, whilst the ablest opponents of the so-called new education,
recognized the claims of physical science to a fair share in any
course of education. Extremists there were, who, with Herbert Spencer, held that the value of the study of the ancient

languages was almost purely conventional, or only quasi-intrinsic, and that there is no discipline given by them not derivable from the sciences, and that "it would be utterly contrary to the beautiful economy of nature if one kind of culture were needed for the gaining of information, and another kind were needed as a mental gymnastic." Others, notably President White, of Cornell University, considered modern languages fully equivalent as a mental gymnastic to the ancient languages, an opinion decidedly at variance with that of John Stuart Mill, President Porter, and others.

Among the results of the agitation, a system of parallel elective courses of study was developed. At certain stages of the college course, a selection of studies to suit the wants or mental peculiarities of the student is permitted. The plan was not altogether new, but met with more general recognition than at any previous time, and has, to a greater or less extent, been adopted by all the leading American Colleges. In some, as in Harvard, it has been carried to such extremes, that a distinctive college course can not be recognized, whilst into others it has been slowly and grudgingly admitted, and to a comparatively limited extent, as at Yale. At Harvard, Latin and Greek are not required after the Freshman year, whilst at the younger Johns Hopkins University, only Latin is required for admission, and no Latin or Greek is required in the course for the Bachelor's degree.

Whilst a wide range of elective studies in an institution may present advantages to some, it requires most ample endowment and large, accumulated libraries, and educational appliances, to carry out, efficiently, such a plan, and even then a large number of students, not only to justify it, but to give it character. It is sometimes called a university plan, and whilst at Harvard it may be so termed with some degree of propriety, and that institution may be in transition to something more than an overgrown college, the actual state of the case is, that there is, to some extent, university liberty of election, without the corresponding antecedent maturity and discipline requisite to judicious election.   Within much narrower limits every decided advantage of elective studies may be obtained, and the course be adapted to the best interests of the student.

At the time of the change in the administration of the Scientific Department, rendered necessary by the death of Professor Wilson, in 1865, the modification of the College course had become a matter of very general consideration.   At the first annual meeting of the Board of Trustees, after his death, in June, 1865, a committee of that body, of which Bishop Simpson was chairman, was appointed to take into consideration a recommendation in the report of President Johnson in regard to the establishment of an enlarged elective course in Biblical Science and Literature, and in Natural Science.   The recommendation of this committee for the establishment of an enlarged course of studies, as soon as the funds of the College would allow, and the granting of discretionary power to the Faculty, " to substitute studies as equivalent in culture," was adopted by the Trustees.   At the same time, the writer, then resident in Germany, pursuing scientific studies, was called to the chair of Natural Science.   Immediately after the death of Professor Wilson, President Johnson had made a request, on behalf of himself and the Faculty, to allow his name to be presented for the position, accompanied by the statement that his old instructor and friend, Professor Wilson, in speaking of his successor, had expressed a similar wish, and among the suggestions in reply was one, that the privilege of election of scientific studies, in lieu of Latin and Greek, in the Junior and Senior years, might add interest and efficiency to the College. With an incumbent in the chair so heartily in accord with the views of the administration of the College, it seemed but nat-

ural that the new plan should have a fair trial. The faculty
determined that practical scientific studies might be substituted
for the Greek of the Junior year, and for the Latin and Greek
of the Senior year, and that the students so electing should be
graduated with the usual degree of Bachelor of Arts. One af-
ternoon of laboratory work was thus considered equivalent to
two recitations per week in the ancient languages. The expansion of the course was thus purely elective. The required
natural science remained as in the old curriculum, namely,
three recitations and two lectures per week for the Junior and
Senior classes, throughout the year, distributed among the
branches usually included under that term.

In the absence of any appropriation for fitting up or equip-
ing a laboratory for this course, the action of the Board was
rather permissive than mandatory. A laboratory, to accom-
modate about a dozen students, was, however, fitted up on the
ground floor of South College, not with all the modern appliances, to be sure, but simply adapted to a rudimentary course
in analytical chemistry. The places were all filled at once.
The inconveniences, deficiencies, and discomforts of the laboratory were cheerfully endured by these pioneers, and all efforts in their behalf were supplemented by earnest and enthusiastic work. The results of the year, as reported to the Trustees
at their annual meeting in 1866, were such as induced them,
after careful consideration, to formally adopt the plan upon
which the department had been conducted during the year. A
more suitable room on the main floor of South College was
granted for laboratory purposes. The necessary funds were
provided for, by a charge of twenty-five dollars per year upon
each student pursuing the course, to cover all expenses for apparatus, chemicals, and so forth. At the same time, the desirability of better and more ample accommodations for the department was admitted. The course, since then, has been con-

ducted essentially on the same basis. The College was thus among the very earliest to inaugurate such a course. Whatever doubts may have existed then, as to its judiciousness, have vanished with its trial, and almost every college has ventured as far, and many further, in the same direction. A fair proportion of the graduates, since that date, are representatives of it, and their success in the various professions, as well as in purely scientific pursuits, does not indicate that the change was unwise or detrimental to intellectual discipline.

Unquestionably many friends of the college hoped by this change to meet more fully the wants of some of its patrons by imparting a more practical character to a part of the course, but an estimate of its usefulness, based for most part on such a view, would be far from correct. The modification was not one so much of amount of study as of improvement in the mode of instruction, and the estimation of its value is connected with the whole subject of scientific studies in a course of liberal education. The place these branches occupy in such a course, must be regulated by the same considerations that assign the place to any other branch of study, namely, the degree and kind of discipline effected, and the value of the knowledge imparted. The direct utility of much of the scientific knowledge imparted is so obvious as well as so great in comparison with that of many other branches, that its disciplinary value may be overlooked. The statement of John Stuart Mill, one of the most uncompromising advocates of discipline, as a chief end of education, and of the ancient languages as a means to it, that "a man totally ignorant of these things, be he ever so skilled in a special profession, is not an educated man, but an ignoramus" is perhaps not too strong, and coupled with the other statement, that "there is no intellectual discipline more important than that which the experimental sciences afford," exhibits the educational rank of these sciences.

The selection of the branches of Natural Science for the purpose of education, as well as the determination of the amount, must be controlled by the same considerations of the knowledge imparted, and of discipline effected. But the obliteration of sharp dividing lines in science has so continually attended its advance, that it is even more difficult' to say what branches of it may be totally ignored, than to establish a minimum in any branch for a man who is to be designated as liberally educated. In fact, the branches are so inter-dependent, that to know one thoroughly, or even passably, something must be known of all. By something, is not meant a few isolated facts or vague impressions or a superficial knowledge, but a general knowledge as distinguished from minute knowledge, a knowledge of the leading facts and principles, of the salient features of the science, but as far as it goes, a thorough knowledge. Such a knowledge will enable any one to follow with intelligent interest the progress of science, and together with its accompanying training, would not be without direct value in professional life. The lawyer might more readily avail himself of the assistance of a scientific expert, the minister of the Gospel might acquire the additional influence of a fuller sympathy with all the pursuits of life, as well as be preserved from scientific inaccuracies in the pulpit. Against the latter, from which he is so singularly free himself, Bishop Simpson saw fit to caution young ministers in his Yale lectures.

But if, as is contended, the discipline effected by the study of the ancient languages can be accomplished by no other studies, in a much higher degree is the discipline imparted by the study of the physical sciences peculiar to them. To say nothing of the cultivation of the faculty of observation, the distinction as drawn by Mill, that "as the classical literature furnishes the most perfect types of expression, so do the physical sciences those of the art of thinking," indicates a more important educational function. All the practical judgments of life, upon which human actions are based, are the result of mental processes similar to those called into play in the investigation of nature, and the rational study of physical science. Science is applied inductive logic, and of course, in order to elicit all its educational value, it must be taught as science not as a mass facts, and more for the science at times than for the facts. President Porter, in assigning the place to physics in a college curriculum, clearly indicates the distinction between the two objects of its study: "to give power over nature, real power as we wield and apply her forces, and intellectual, as we interpret her secrets, predict her phenomena, enforce her laws, and recreate her universe."

But the real fruitfulness of the knowledge acquired, as well as the accompanying mental discipline, depends more upon the manner of its acquisition than upon its amount. It must not be mere cram that scarcely survives the day of examination. It may not, indeed, be altogether the most available for a formal examination. It must be organizable knowledge, so assimilated that it is always at command. The three methods of teaching Natural Science, by text-book and recitations, by lectures, accompanied by experimental illustrations, and by experiments and investigations performed by the student himself, are so different in character that they can hardly be compared as to efficiency, and they supplement each other so fully that they should, as far as possible, accompany each other. The text-book, when used by itself, yields the poorest return in most cases for the time and drudgery of both student and instructor, but in its proper connection its use imparts fullness and precision, and conduces to facility in reference. The latter may be of the greatest value in after life, and in the investigation of any subject would be of far more value than a memory crammed with facts. Recitations upon the text-book

also afford the largest opportunity to the instructor for the cor-
rection of defective methods of study and carelessness in reading; for the best of students recite as they read; and misap-
prehension in reading is as common as ambiguity in expression. Whilst it requires but little time for the experienced
teacher to ascertain to what extent a student may have mastered a subject, it is more tedious and difficult to obtain a
careful, and clearly and properly expressed statement of what
is known, and that only by refusing to understand any other.
This method possesses an additional advantage in fostering a
familiarity, by frequent use, with the fittest words, not strictly
technical, for scientific statements, an acquisition certainly as
desirable, and worth as much effort as the accumulation of a
Greek or Latin vocabulary, which can seldom be used without
an air of pedantry.

But however excellent the text-book, the necessity for experimental lectures in connection with it has always been recognized for the vitalization of the facts there formulated in
words. Not every fact, of course, need be objectively reproduced to be clearly comprehended, but by the selection of
facts of a typical character for reproduction the comprehension of many may be aided. If the body of facts, therefore,
taught by means of lectures alone would be meager, their arrangement may differ from the almost unavoidable encyclo-
pædic plan of the text-book, especially if it is to be regarded
as a book of reference, and general principles can be more
clearly taught, and the reasoning processes employed in scientific investigations can be more fully exhibited, and besides the
discipline and encouragement in the use of the faculty of observation involved, they also serve best to point out the path
to science and to indicate its domain.

These two methods were exclusively employed at the time
of the enlargement of the course. Its expansion did not

consist in the increase of amount of text-book, or in number
of lectures, but by the addition of the third method of experiment and investigation by the student. This method is
to the lectures almost what the lectures are to the text-book.
The student is no longer merely a passive recipient of
truth, the lecturer telling him this and showing him that, but
he is in the condition of an intelligent agent eliciting truth;
he does not simply witness the lecturer questioning nature
by experiment, and receive the replies at second hand, as
interpreted by the lecturer, but with the instruments in his own
hands, he addresses the questions himself, he is obliged to observe, distinguish, compare, and value facts; he begins to realize how much that is essential to the success of an experiment,
or to successful investigation of nature, is necessarily left un-
said or unexposed by a lecturer, how multitudinous the essential conditions of even the humblest experiment frequently are,
how the minutest and apparently most trifling one is just as
essential to success as the most prominent, and withal how
much of individual experience that can not be written, or expressed, or communicated in any way, must be mixed up with
the most detailed directions that may be given. He will at once
encounter two difficulties similar to those that one with but a
smattering of the language at first encounters in a foreign land—
a difficulty first in asking questions, and then, if he happens to
be successful, an equally great, more annoying, and perhaps
mortifying inability to understand the rapid reply in sounds
unfamiliar to the ear. The student thus prosecuting scientific
studies not only has the facts ground into his memory more in-
erasably, but, what is even better, he is brought to realize the
difficulties that beset the investigation of nature, he comes to
understand more fully the unexpressed uncertainties and inaccuracies, and the unavoidable errors that attach to statements

of scientific facts, as well as the misinterpretations of them that may be made.

There was no model upon which to adjust a course to the new requirements. A rudimentary course in chemical analysis presented itself as one most readily adapted to the case. The apparatus required is simple, inexpensive, and easily manipulated, whilst the reasoning involved is easily followed, and it is capable of variation to meet different cases. In the absence of a suitable American text-book at that time, the well-known Giessen tables, by Professor Will, were translated and published for the class, and in so far met a similar want that soon was felt in other institutions, that a second enlarged edition was called for. The general outline of chemical analysis furnished by them was supplemented by the fuller works on analytical chemistry placed in the laboratory for reference by the student. It was soon found that the course could be varied with advantage in many cases, after some of the awkwardness in manipulation and in reasoning from facts had disappeared, by the substitution of subjects in general chemistry and physics, which required a wider range of information, more complicated apparatus, and greater skill in manipulation. Such higher privileges accorded, to such as are prepared to enjoy them, are calculated not only to act as an incentive to application, but also to mitigate the somewhat Procrustean character of the treatment of students involved in the class system. Thus, whilst a minimum of study and proficiency is required of every student, there is no limit in the other direction but the natural ability, application and disposition of the student.

The course is not, however, made exclusively elective. Students in other courses, of superior ability and proficiency in their studies are allowed an opportunity to utilize a portion of their leisure time in laboratory practice as extra work, with a note of the fact in the catalogue, and the claim to a certificate of it. With increased experience and increased facilities, new opportunities and new incentives for study are introduced. There is, of course, no expectation in this way to turn out Bachelors of Arts as chemists, &c., but simply to make these branches of a liberal education as thorough as the times seem to demand, and to afford a good foundation, if desired, for subsequent scientific pursuits. Each student in the laboratory is provided with a desk, apparatus, chemicals, and the use of text-books, for an annual charge of twenty-five dollars. No additional charges are made, except in cases of gross carelessness or negligence. General books of reference and the leading scientific journals are also accessible to the students. Any student sufficiently proficient in the language is allowed to use text-books and books of reference in German. Exercises for practice are arranged in qualitative analysis, including the use of the blow-pipe, and the determination of the commoner minerals; in quantitative analysis of ores, volumetric and gravimetric; urinary analysis; toxicology and photographic chemistry, and also an experimental course in physics, by the student, including experiments in light, electricity, sound, heat, lantern projections, the use of the spectroscope, photometer, camera, &c. A Teacher's Course is also arranged for the benefit of those who may desire to give instruction in natural science, which embraces instruction in the use and care of apparatus employed for illustration in natural philosophy and chemistry, and the performance, by means of the simplest and least expensive apparatus, of the experiments adapted to the instruction of classes in those branches. As a part of the course in the second year the students are obliged to deliver experimental lectures before the classes, organized as a society, under its regulations, and also to make use of scientific periodicals, as is more fully explained in connection with the operations of the Scientific Society.

The course in photography includes the collodion process, wet and dry, silver and carbon printing, the emulsion process, the preparation of photographic chemicals, the recovery of photographic waste, &c. In all cases the production of results is subordinated to a thorough study of the principles involved. Perhaps no application of science is better adapted to discipline the eye, impart delicacy in manipulation, and impress the student more forcibly with the necessity for attention to the minutest details, whilst its almost numberless and rapidly increasing applications may render it of practical value outside of purely scientific applications or amateur practice at any time.

As to the general mode of instruction, the student upon his entrance into the laboratory, must be relieved of some very natural erroneous notions and expectations. It does not afford a royal road to knowledge. Experiments, unmixed with earnest thought, amount to but little. Following a plan of operations mechanically to a result, is not scientific investigation, and when the current becomes too even it must be disturbed by the quiet interjection of some obstacle. Perfect willingness to repeat failures, occasioned by hurried manipulation or carelessness at the tenth and final stage, as often as may be required, without a murmur, is not scientific patience. It is a very different quality from that manifested in the uniform, sustained attention, and care at all points, with no weak intervals, which renders repetition unnecessary. Haste and carelessness in reading are as prolific of failures as haste in working. By obliging the student to read, do, observe, and conclude for himself, and simply starting him over the beaten path of failure again and again, with perhaps a caution on some points, he may be led to realize—some sooner, others later—the meaning of the term patience, or of that "transcendent capacity for taking trouble," which Carlyle placed as the first element of genius, and it will be learned for life.

CHAPTER XIV.

SCIENTIFIC SOCIETY.

ORGANIZATION — SEAL—EXERCISES — EFFICIENCY—CONSTITUTION AND BY-LAWS—REGULATION OF EXERCISES—PHOTOGRAPHS BY THE SOCIETY — DIRECTOR — LECTURES BY THE STUDENT, MODE OF PREPARATION AND DISCIPLINARY VALUE—VALUE OF SCIENTIFIC PERIODICALS.

N 1867, the students pursuing this course organized themselves into a society, under the name of the "Scientific Society of Dickinson College," with the expressed wish to extend their knowledge of the various branches of natural science, and to provide facilities for their thorough study.

The device of the seal, a ray of light from a star, decomposed by a prism, and the motto, *Nunc ad Sidera*, were intended to mark the cosmical character then but recently imparted to chemistry by the spectroscope. As the society proposed to it-

self the very modest aim of simply extending the knowledge
of its members, and made no pretensions to adding to the sum
total of human knowledge, its exercises and conduct were confined exclusively to that purpose. They have been varied,
from time to time, and, in many cases, have been merely ten-
tative, and whilst its efficiency has varied with the character,
enthusiasm, and numbers of its members, it has, at all times,
proved an important addition to the ordinary methods of instruction, and seems full of still larger possibilities for the improvement and inspiration of the student connected with it.
All that has proved valuable in the working of the society, in
its first ten years, is embodied in its recent constitution and by-
laws. After providing for the usual officers and for the election of members, Corresponding and Honorary, as well as
active, the more specific measures for carrying out the objects
of the society, are stated in an article, which prescribes that
" the exercises of the society shall consist of lectures by the
members, accompanied by illustrative experiments; reports of
laboratory work; written and verbal communications upon scientific subjects, including reviews of, and abstracts from, scientific or other periodicals; and criticism of the regular perform-
ances of the members. The by-laws are, for the most part,
concerned with carrying out this article on exercises. The
subject of lectures must be announced a week in advance.
The lectures must be accompanied by illustrative experiments,
must be delivered without manuscript, except brief notes, and
are restricted to twenty minutes, unless the time is extended by
a vote of the society. The critic is appointed a week before,
and is expected to study up the subject, and criticism includes
the subject, subject matter, facts, arrangement, mode of treatment, and experimental treatment and details. A Scientific
Reporter is also appointed, from time to time, whose duty it is
to examine carefully the scientific and other periodicals for

items of interest, and call the attention of the society to them by verbal statements, written abstracts, or experiments. There are other provisions of an equally practical character, including the division of the society into sections, one of which, on photography, has the matter of the photographic publications of the society in charge. The published list of these includes, in addition to views of the College grounds, &c., photographs of apparatus, of scientific men, of charts, &c. Under supervision of the committee on lectures, music was, on one occasion, during a public lecture, received from Philadelphia, and at another the phonograph was exhibited and explained.

Perhaps the most unique feature of the constitution is, however, the provision for an officer called the Director. The Professor of Chemistry fills this place *ex-officio*. This is a piece of mechanism to carry the organization past dead points. If the society intermits from any cause, or its organization becomes deranged, the power is lodged with him to call meetings for reorganization, &c., as well as to call extra meetings when the interests of the society may require. Many a society of similar character has passed quietly out of existence for want of just some such provision.

A prize, called the Scientific Society's Prize, is given to the member of the Senior Class who may give the fullest and most scientific account of experiments made upon some subject selected by the Society.

The lectures before the society by the students, which are required as part of the course, have a discipline peculiarly their own. He is expected to select his subject from a list suggested by the professor, or elsewhere if he desires, to make himself master of it, to select his mode of treatment, prepare his notes, make out a list of his experiments, put in a requisition for the apparatus needed, and after he has done all that can be expected of him, his mode of treatment may not be the best, the experi-

9

ments selected may not be well adapted to it or to each other, and the apparatus may be ideal rather than practical, but what he presents is his own, and its preparation will have involved an excellent discipline, and form a basis upon which advice and instruction may be given without enfeebling. Its delivery from notes alone, with the manipulatory details, tends to develop the power of many sided attention as well as readiness in expression.

The careful examination of the leading scientific periodicals, and the study of such articles, especially of original research, as fall within the student's range of acquirements, is encouraged not only on account of their superiority in freshness and interest to the text-book, but because of the familiarity thus produced, with the style in which original investigations and observations of any character are best narrated.

CHAPTER XV.

SOUTH COLLEGE AND PROPOSED NEW SCIENTIFIC BUILDING.

SOUTH COLLEGE—DESIRABILITY OF A NEW BUILDING SUGGESTED—APPROVED BY THE TRUSTEES—SCOPE, CHARACTER, AND LOCATION OF IT—MEETING IN WASHINGTON, D. C.—PLANS OF BUILDING. PROSPECTS.

SOUTH College, originally built as a church, was burned down in December, 1836, and re-built on its original foundation, and was exclusively used for the purposes of the Grammar School until 1846, when the College library, the museum, the lecture room of natural science, and laboratory were removed to it from West College. In 1865, the Grammar School was removed to West College,

and the library and museum were removed to the third floor, to make room for the laboratory, adjoining the lecture room. The building, although not in good repair, presents quite an agreeable general exterior, but owing to its construction upon a plan designed for entirely different purposes, a great portion of it cannot be utilized, at present, to advantage. The lecture-room and laboratory are comfortable in size and well lighted, but according to the report of Professor of Natural Science in 1878, the department has reached the limit of its growth and efficiency with its present accommodations. More room is needed to properly house and care for, and satisfactorily use the additional appliances the College should have, and the institution is also losing, each day, opportunities for the collection of valuable educational material for want of a larger and more suitable building. With such a building provided, any deficiencies in equipment could easily be removed. The rooms, at present occupied by the college library and the museum, are not in keeping with these two great interests of the College. With the college library and those of the two societies massed in a suitable room, not only would the thirty thousand volumes be more available for study, but would also form a juster impression of the resources of the College in this particular, whilst the museum, with the encouragement of proper apartments, could easily be rendered as complete as might be desired for the purposes of instruction.

Whilst the department, therefore, is not suffering at present, it has been thought advisable to make an effort to provide for the very near future. A suggestion in the same report that such a building, with proper and united effort, could be completed by the centennial of the College, in 1883, was received with favor by the Trustees, and a resolution was passed by them authorizing Professor Himes to raise the sum of $25,000, for the erection of such a building, and pledging their hearty coöperation. According to another part of the same report, it was urged that the building should be a building not for the sake of a building, but for the sake of its uses, and to meet the wants of the College, as a college—should have ample provision for at least two professors in the department, and should, therefore, contain two lecture rooms, two laboratories for students—one chemical, the other physical—two offices and private laboratories for the professors, and the necessary rooms for apparatus, &c., in both cases. For the present, at least, it should also contain accommodations for the library as well the museum. The College is fortunate in the possession of a beautiful lot of ground on Main street, ninety feet by two hundred and forty feet, unsurpassed in adaptation for a building for scientific purposes. It has a fine open exposure on all sides, and ample opportunities for sunlight, so essential at this time, in many cases, for investigations and instruction in physical science, and withal it is of such a character that a highly creditable building in appearance could be erected with the least outlay, and without any necessity for the sacrifice of internal room or convenience for merely external display.

Plans have not yet been fully matured for bringing the matter before the friends of the College. At an informal meeting of friends of the College, including some leading scientific men and educators, as well as alumni, called together in Washington, to consult in regard to measures for the furtherance of the project, the state of the Scientific Department of the College was represented by Professor Himes, and the opinion expressed that any plan of building proposed should be for purely collegiate purposes; that a weak university was not necessarily a strong college, and that it should be formed exclusively with reference to the scientific uses to which the building was to be put. Very valuable suggestions were made by Professor Baird, of the Smithsonian Institution, of the class of

1840, and formerly a Professor in the College, as also by Professor Remsen, of the Johns Hopkins University. The latter especially dwelt upon the desirability of a building exclusively for scientific purposes, in preference to large monumental buildings for all purposes. The importance of extreme care in the preparation of a plan for a building of the kind proposed seemed, after a free interchange·of opinions, to be so great, in order to avoid the defects and inconsistencies so frequently met with in buildings erected for scientific purposes, often at great cost, that Professor Baird, Hon. M. G. Emory, and Professor Himes were requested to prepare a plan, to be submittted to the Board of Trustees.

Although the time was entirely consumed with the consideration of the above more immediate objects of the meeting, there were incidental indications that when the enterprise is properly brought before the friends of the College there will be no failure for financial reasons, and that before the Centennial of the College, in 1883, its wants in this respect will be fully met.

CHAPTER XVI.

CONCLUSION.

OR details of facilities for instruction, courses of study, and information of a similar character, the announcements made with the annual catalogues of the College may be consulted. They may, however, be recapitulated in brief, as buildings ample for collegiate purposes, set in a Campus of unrivaled beauty, libraries in the aggregate containing nearly thirty thousand volumes, philosophical apparatus extensive and annually increasing, collections in natural history that, with proper room for use and display, would be of great value for purposes of instruction, including a beautiful collection of minerals bequeathed to the College by Samuel Ashmead, Esq., of Philadelphia; an observatory armed with an excellent achromatic telescope, with an objective five inches in diameter, of seven feet focal length, and equatorially mounted, and adapted to research as well as instruction; a reading-room, commodious and well lighted, and supplied with a wide range of current literature, &c.

The work of the College is restricted to two courses of study, the one the usual regular course of four years of the best American Colleges for the degree of Bachelor of Arts, with limited election in the Junior and Senior years; the other a Latin-Scientific course, which, on account of the omission of Greek, can be completed in three years, and entitles the student to the degree of Bachelor of Philosophy. Although students are permitted to pursue a partial course selected out of the other courses, without being candidates for graduation, such cases are exceptional, and require special action and consent of the Faculty.

The location of the College is one of the most favorable in the middle section of our country. The Cumberland Valley is unsurpassed in beauty, fertility, and healthiness, whilst the inland situation of the town of Carlisle exempts the students from many temptations to vice and extravagance found in the larger cities. Connected by the Cumberland Valley railroad, one of the oldest and best in the country, with the city of Harrisburg, eighteen miles distant, the great railroad center of the State, it is readily accessible from Baltimore, Philadelphia, and other points, whilst other roads projected, and doubtless soon to be completed, will open up new routes to Baltimore and the south-west. The marked contrast in this particular of the present with the earlier days of the College suggests itself. To refer again to Chief Justice Taney's narrative: It required him two weeks to make the journey from his home, in Calvert county, Maryland, to Carlisle; as there was no stage-coach or other public conveyance at that time between Baltimore and Carlisle, he and his companion were obliged to wait at an inn in Baltimore, until a wagon could be found returning to Carlisle, not too heavily laden to take their trunks and allow them to ride occasionally, and they were obliged to carry money in specie sufficient to cover their expenses until the next vacation, placed at considerable risks in their trunks, often left in the open wagon in the public wagon-yard; he only visited his home twice during his college course, in both cases performing the journey on foot to Baltimore in two days. Even in 1833, the leading men of the Methodist Conferences in its first Board of Trustees reached the town in the old stage-coaches converging upon it from different directions. It is somewhat singular that this highly objectionable inaccessibility

of a literary institution, now so happily overcome by the wonderful progress of half a century, did not prevail against the
establishment of the College, or even against its later adoption
by the Methodist Church.

The present condition of the College may be described as
full of encouragement to its friends.   It seems more firmly established than at any previous period of its history.   Without
debt, with resources sufficient to carry on all the college work
creditably, with a promise of a steady, healthy increase in the
number of its students, with projected improvements likely to be
realized, with 'evidences of newly awakened interest on every
side, among the friends of education in the Conferences and its
Alumni, frequently manifested in inquiries as to the plans for
the celebration of its rapidly approaching centennial, there is
every reason to hope that it will soon fully recover the proud
position it once occupied.

Its fifty years of history, in connection with the Methodist
Episcopal Church, have been the most flourishing, as well as
highly creditable to that denomination, and are filled with
associations and memories that must continue to deepen the
hold of the College upon it, whilst its continual contributions of Alumni to its various fields of labor, indicate the
high place that it fills in the economy of that Church.   One
of its most honored bishops, its senior missionary secretary,
the President of its leading theological seminary, many of the
pastors of its leading churches, suggest themselves at once
among her prominent sons, whilst in the preparation of the
Biblical and Theological Library, ordered by the General Conference of 1872, both editors are graduates of Dickinson, two
of the leading volumes are assigned to sons of the same family,
and the first of the series to appear, admittedly a credit, not
only to the Church, but to the country, comes directly from
the College itself.   In its long, unbroken line of Alumni are

found many eminent in all positions in life, including a President of the United States, as well as a Chief Justice, Judges, Senators, Congressmen, Cabinet Officers, and professional men of high rank. To quote the words of one of the highly honored "first Faculty:" "Happy is the mother who has reared such sons. When the hundredth anniversary of the opening of Dickinson College shall arrive, let her living Alumni come up from all parts of the country, and from the four quarters of the earth, and gather around her hearth-stone to rejoice together, and to pledge anew their fidelity to culture, patriotism, and religion, to one another, and to Alma Mater. Let them come with full hearts and hands, and pour into her lap such offerings as shall place her where her founders meant she should stand—in the front rank of American colleges."

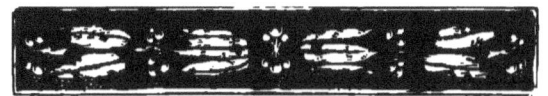

CHAPTER XVI.

TRUSTEES OF DICKINSON COLLEGE.

Elected.	(Clergymen marked *.)	Ceased.
1783,	John Dickinson, LL. D.,	1808
1783,	Henry Hill,	1798
1783,	James Wilson, LL. D.,	1798
1783,	William Bingham,	1804
1783,	Benjamin Rush, M. D., LL. D.,	1813
1783,	James Boyd,	1787
1783,	John McDowell,	1825
1783,	Henry Ernest Muhlenberg, D. D.,*	1815
1783,	William Hendel,*	1802
1783,	James Jacks,	1802
1783,	John Black,*	1802
1783,	Alexander Dobbin,*	1809
1783,	John McKnight, D. D.,*	1794
1783,	James Ewing,	1810
1783,	Robert McPherson,	1789
1783,	Henry Slagle,	1810
1783,	Thomas Hartley,	1801
1783,	Michael Hahn,	1792
1783,	John King, D. D.,*	1813
1783,	Robert Cooper, D. D.,*	1805
1783,	James Lang,*	1798
1783,	Samuel Waugh,*	1807
1783,	William Linn, D. D.,*	1787
1783,	John Linn,*	1821

138

Elected.		Censed.
1783,	. . . John G. Armstrong, ...	. . . 1794
1783,	. . . John Montgomery, ...	. . . 1808
1783,	. . . Stephen Duncan, ...	. . . 1794
1783,	. . . Thomas Smith, ...	. . . 1809
1783,	. . . Robert Magaw, ...	. . . 1790
1783,	. . Samuel A. McCoskry, ...	. . . 1815
1783,	. . Christopher Emanuel Shulze,*	. . 1788
1783,	. . . Peter Spyker, ...	. . . 1794
1783,	. . John Arndt, ...	. . . 1788
1783,	. . . William Montgomery, ...	. . . 1794
1783,	. . . William Maclay, ...	. . . 1796
1783,	. . . Barnard Dougherty, ...	. . . 1792
1883,	. . . David Espy, ...	. . . 1795
1783,	. . . James Sutton,*	. . . 1784
1783,	. . . Alexander McClean, ...	. . . 1788
1783,	. . . William McCleery, ...	. . . 1788
1784,	. . . Nicholas Kurtz,*	. . . 1796
1787,	. . . Joseph Montgomery,*	. . . 1794
1787,	. . James Latta, D. D.,*	. . . 1801
1788,	. . William Irvine, ...	. . . 1803
1788,	. . . Robert Johnston, ...	. . . 1808
1788,	. . . Patrick Alison, D. D.,*	. . . 1788
1788,	. . . James Snodgrass,*	. . 1833
1788,	. . . John Creigh, ...	. . . 1813
1789,	. . . Joseph Thornbury, ...	. . . 1799
1790,	. . . Thomas Duncan, LL. D., ...	. . 1816
1792,	. . . George Stevenson, ...	. . . 1827
1792,	. . . Ephraim Blaine, ...	. . 1804
1794,	. . . Robert Cathcart, D. D.,*	. . . 1833
1794,	. . . Nathaniel R. Snowden,*	1827
1794,	. . . Samuel Laird, ...	. . . 1807
1794,	. . Charles McClure, ...	. . . 1811

Elected.		Ceased.
1784, . .	James Hamilton,	. . . 1820
1794, . . .	Michael Ege, . .	1815
1795, . . .	Samuel Weakley, ...	1821
1796, . . .	John Campbell, D. D.,* .	. . . 1820
1796, . . .	James Armstrong, . .	 1826
1798, . . .	Thomas McPherrin,* . . . . '. . . . 1802
1798, . . .	James Riddle, , ...	 1833
1798, . . .	Francis Gurney, . .	 1815
1799, . . .	Charles Smith, LL. D.,	 1824
1801, . . .	David Denny,* 1833
1801, . . .	David Watts, ... 1820
1802, . . .	Joshua Williams, D. D.,* 1821
1802, . .	John Young,* 1803
1802,	Robert Coleman, ... 1826
1802, . . .	David McConaughy, D. D.,* 1834
1803, . . .	Hugo H. Brackenridge, ... 1816
1803, . . .	Francis Herron, D. D.,* 1816
1804, . . .	Jonathan Walker, ... 1824
1805, . . .	Nathan Grier,* 1814
1807, . .	Jonathan Helfenstein,* 1826
1807, · · ·	James Duncan, ... 1808
1808, . . .	James Gustine, ... 1820
1808, . . .	William Alexander, ... 1814
1808, . . .	Jacob Hendel, ... 1833
1807, . . .	Robert Davidson, D. D.,* 1812
1809, . . .	William M. Brown, ... 1827
1811, . . .	Robert Blaine, ... 1826
1814, . . .	Andrew Carothers, ... 1833
1814, . . .	John Lind,* 1825
1814, . . .	Francis Pringle,* 1828
1815, . . .	Nathaniel Chapman, M. D., ... 1833
1815, . . .	Edward James Stiles, ... 1827

Elected.		Ceased.
1815,	. . John McKnight, D. D.,*	1820
1815,	. . . Albert Helfenstein,*	1826
1815,	. . . George A. Lyon, ...	1833
1816,	. . . John Bannister Gibson, LL. D., . .	1829
1816,	. . . Amos Ellmaker, ...	1821
1820,	. . George Duffield,*	1833
1820,	. . . Henry R. Wilson,*	1825
1820,	. . John Swartzwelder,*	1825
1820,	. . . Isaiah Graham, ...	1834
1820,	. . John Moodey,*	1834
1820,	. . . Isaac B. Parker, ...	1833
1820,	. . . Alexander Mahon, ...	1827
1820,	. . . Joseph Knox, ...	1827
1820,	. . . William N. Irvine, ...	1833
1820,	. . . Jacob Alter, ...	1823
1820,	. . . Andrew Boden, ...	1827
1821,	. . . William R. DeWitt, D. D.,*	1834
1821,	. . . John Reed, LL. D., ...	1828
1821,	. . . John S. Ebaugh,*	1833
1821,	. . . William C. Chambers, M. D., ...	1833
1823,	. . . Ashbel Green, D. D., LL. D., ...	1826
1824,	. . . Michael Ege, ...	1827
1824,	. . . Benjamin Keller,*	1833
1824,	. . . John F. Grier, D. D.,*	1829
1824,	. . James Hamilton, ...	1833
1825,	. . . George Lochman, D. D.,*	1826
1825,	. George Metzger, ...	1833
1825,	. . . John D. Mahon, ...	1834
1826,	. . . Redmond Conyngham, ...	1827
1826,	. . . Benjamin Stiles, ...	1827
1826,	. . . Richard Rush, ...	1832
1827,	. . . David Elliott, D. D.,*	1829

Elected.		Ceased.
1827,	. . John Nevin, ...	1830
1827,	. . Samuel Agnew, M. D., ...	1832
1827,	. . . John McClure, ...	1833
1827,	. . . John Creigh, ...	1833
1827,	George Chambers, ...	1834
1827,	. . . Charles Bingham Penrose, ...	1833
1827,	. . . Samuel Alexander, ...	1833
1828,	. . . Samuel S. Schmucker, D. D.,*	1833
1828,	. . . Calvin Blythe, ...	1833
1828,	. . . Frederick Watts, ...	1833
1828,	. . Gabriel Hiester, ...	1833
1828,	. . . James Coleman, ...	1833
1829,	. . Jacob M. Haldeman, ...	1833
1829,	Samuel Baird, ...	1833
1829,	. . . John Paxton, M. D., ...	1833
1829,	. . . Alexander Fridge, ...	1833
1829,	. . John V. E. Thorn,*	1833
1830,	. . . Alexander Nisbet, ...	1833
1831,	. . Jesse Duncan Elliott, ...	1833
1833,	. . . John Emory, D. D., Bishop M. E. Church,	1836
1833,	. . . John McLean, LL. D., ...	1855
1833,	. . . Stephen G. Roszel,*	1841
1833,	. . Joseph Lybrand,*	1844
1833,	. . . Alfred Griffith,*	1869
1833,	. . . Samuel Harvey, ...	1848
1833,	. . . Job Guest,*	1836
1833,	. . . Henry Antes, ...	1840
1833,	. Theodore Myers, M. D., ...	1839
1833,	. . . John M. Keagy, M. D., ...	1835
1833,	. . . Samuel Baker, M. D., ...	1836
1833,	. . John Davis, ...	1843
1833,	. . . John Phillips, ...	1860

Elected.		Ceased.
1833, . . .	Matthew Anderson, M. D.,	 1838
1833, . . .	Ira Day, M. D., ...	. . . 1866
1833, . .	Richard Benson.	 1844
1833, . . .	Thomas Sewall, M. D.,	 1845
1833. . . .	Henry Hicks, ...	. . . 1837
1833,	George W. Nabb, .	. . . 1840
1833, . . .	Samuel H. Higgins,	. . 1837
1833, . . .	Charles A. Warfield, . . .	 1837
1833, .	James Roberts, ...	 1835
1833, . .	James Dunlop, ...	. . . 1839
1833. . . .	Benjamin Matthias, ...	1850
1833, .	Charles McClure,	. . . 1846
1833, ...	Samuel E. Parker, ...	. . . 1835
1833, .	William M. Biddle, ...	. . . 1855
1833, .	Thomas A. Budd, ...	. . . 1843
1833, .	Thomas E. Bond, M. D.,	 1835
1833, . . .	James B. Longacre,	 1869
1833, . . .	Joseph Holdich, D. D.,*	 1835
1833, . . .	Charles Pitman, D. D.,*	1854
1834, . .	Henry Boehm,* . .	 1838
1834, . . .	William Hamilton,*	. 1838
1834, . . .	James Watson, ...	. . . 1839
1834, . .	John Harper, ...	. . 1847
1834, . . .	James Massey,	 1837
1834, . . .	Charles F. Mayer,	 1836
1835, . . .	Thomas Chapman Thornton,* .	 1837
1835, . .	Joseph S. Carson, ...	. . 1864
1835, . .	Solomon Higgins,*	1838
1835, . . .	Matthew Sorin,*	. . 1838
1835, . . .	Thomas Jefferson Thompson, D. D.,	. 1874
1835, . . .	Jacob Weaver, ...	. . . 1850

Elected.		Ceased.
1836, .	. James Osgood Andrew, D. D. Bishop M. E. Church, ...	1839
1836, . .	. Comfort Tiffany, ...	1858
1836, .	. Samuel B. Martin, M. D., ...	1838
1836, .	George Grimston Cookman,*	1846
1837, .	. Samuel Ashmead, ...	1855
1837, . .	Henry Holden, ...	1840
1837, .	. Alexander L. Hays, ...	1841
1837, . .	. James Wright, ...	1859
1837, . .	. Thomas B. Sargent,*	1866
1837, .	. John A. Elkinton, M. D., ...	1840
1838, . .	. Richard Battee, ...	1848
1838, . .	. Martin W. Bates, ...	1851
1838, . .	. John S. Porter,*	1855
1838, . .	. Emund S. Janes,*	1839
1838, . .	Manning Force,*	1843
1838, . .	. John Davis,*	1854
1839, . .	. Levi Scott,*	1841
1838, . .	. William D. Seymour, ...	1841
1839, . .	. Robert Morris, ...	1841
1830, . .	. Beverly Waugh, D. D., Bishop M. E. Church,	1858
1839, . .	. James S. Owens, ...	1845
1840, . .	. Jacob Carrigan, ...	1857
1840, . .	. John Herr, ...	1845
1840, . .	. John Buckman, ...	1842
1841, . .	. William Hamilton, D. D.,*	1864
1841, . .	. Robert Emory, D. D.,*	1845
1841, . .	. John Kennaday, D. D.,*	1852
1841, . .	. James Bishop, ...	1861
1841,	Henry Antes, ...	1856
1841, . .	. Frederick Watts, ...	1844
1842, . .	. Charles W. Roberts, ...	1845

Elected.		Ceased.
1843,	. . . Charles B. Tippett,*	. 1867
1843,	. . . Richard W. Dodson, ...	 1847
1843,	. . . Archibald Wright, ... , ...	. 1851
1844,	. . . James J. Boswell, ...	. . 1850
1844,	. Edwin L. Janes,*	. . 1845
1844,	. . . John J. Myers, M. D., . . .	. . 1854
1845,	. . . Thomas Browne, ...	. 1850
1845,	. . . David Creamer,	. . 1865
1845,	. . . Andrew Hay, ...	1857
1845,	. . . Stephen Asbury Roszel,*	. 1852
1845,	. John P. Durbin, D. D., ...	. 1864
1846,	. . . Jesse Bowman, ...	. 1859
1846,	. . Richard H. Carter, ...	. 1848
1847,	. . . Albert J. Ritchie, M. D.,	 1856
1847,	. . . Abraham Herr Smith.	
1848,	. . Daniel Moore Bates, ...	. 1865
1848,	. . . Walker P. Conway, ...	. 1864
1848,	. . . John McClintock, D. D.,*	. 1859
1848,	. . . S. A. Barton, M. D., .	 1864
1850,	. . . William H. Allen, M. D., LL. D., ...	. 1864 .
1850,	. . . John Whiteman.	
1850,	. . . Christian Stayman.	
1850,	. . . John F. Bird, M. D.	
1850,	. . . Spencer F. Baird, D. P. S., ...	. 1857
1851,	. . Alexander Cummings, ...	. 1860
1852,	. . . Francis Hodgson, D. D.,*	. 1877
1852,	. . . Jesse T. Peck, D. D.,*	. . 1856
1854,	. . Aquila A. Reese, D. D.,*	. 1869
1854,	. . . Daniel P. Kidder, D. D., ...	. 1855
1854,	. . . John Tonner, ...	. 1864
1855,	. . . Pennel Coombe.*	
1855,	. . . William H. Miller, ...	. 1877

10

Elected.		Ceased.
1855, . . .	Daniel Pierson.	1857
1855, . . .	Charles Joseph Baker, ...	1864
1856, . . .	N. J. B. Morgan, ...	1858
1856, . . .	Augustus O. Hiester, ...	1875
1856, . . .	John Armstrong Wright.	
1857, . . .	W. E. Tunison,*	1858
1857, . . .	Edwin Wilmer, ...	1870
1857, . . .	John C. Harkness, ...	1859
1857, . . .	John H. Bently, ...	1858
1857, . . .	Benjamin H. Browning, ...	1858
1858, . . .	William E. Perry.*	
1858, . .	John H. Phillips, ...	1869
1858, . . .	George F. Fort, ...	1867
1858, . . .	Samuel A. Williams, M. D., ...	1864
1858, .	Bernard Harrison Nadal, D. D.,*	1869
1858, . . .	Levi Scott, D. D., Bishop M. E. Church.	
1859, . . .	John Carson.	
1859, . . .	William Ryland Woodward.	
1859, . .	Samuel Y. Munroe,*	1865
1859, . .	Jacob Rheem, ...	1878
1860, . . .	S. M. Harrington, ...	1861
1860, . . .	Isaac P. Cook, ...	1869
1861, . . .	James Fowler Rusling.	
1862, . . .	Joseph C. De Lacour, ...	1863
1864, . . .	Matthew Simpson, D. D., Bishop M. E. Church.	
1864, . .	Samuel Norment, ...	1877
1864, . . .	John B. McCreary, ...	1869
1864, . .	Thomas Sewall, D. D.,*	1866
1864, . . .	Francis A. Crook.	
1864, . .	John Patton, ...	1867
1864, . . .	W. H. Edes, ...	1865

Elected.		Ceased.
1864, . .	F. A. Ellis, ...	. . 1877
1864, . . .	William Daniel, ...	1876
1864, . .	Caleb E. Wright, ...	. . 1876
1865, . . .	William Milnes, ...	. 1867
1865, . . .	J. A. J. Creswell, ...	. 1871
1865, . . .	M. G. Emery, ...	. 1878
1865, . . .	Charles H. Whitecar,*	. 1874
1866, . .	George D. Chenoweth,*	. 1874
1866, . . .	R. C. Woodward, ...	. . 1878
1866, . . .	John Lanahan, D. D., ...	. 1869
1867, . . .	Thomas G. Chattle, M. D.	
1867, . .	B. H. Crever,*	. . 1873
1867, . . .	Samuel Hindes, ...	. 1870
1867, . . .	J. B. McEnally, ...	. 1874
1869, .	James A. McCauley, D. D.,*	. 1872
1869, . . .	John S. Deale, D. D.*	
1869, . . .	Charles J. Baker.	
1869, .	A. E. Gibson, M. D., D. D.*	
1869, . . .	John F. Chaplain, D. D.*	
1869, . . .	William H. Bodine.	
1869, . . .	James H. Lightbourne,*	1875
1869, . . .	William H. Shakespeare, ...	1877
1870, .	Walter H. Thompson, ...	1877
1870, . . .	Albert H. Slape.	
1872, . . .	J. B. Quigg.*	
1872, . . .	Thomas W. Eliason, ...	1873
1873, . . .	T. Mitchell, D. D.*	
1873, . . .	Thomas S. Dunning, M. D., ...	1874
1874, . . .	Jonathan Boynton.	
1874, . . .	John Wilson.	
1875, .	Clarence J. Jackson.	
1875, . . .	James Hunter.	

Elected.		Ceased.
1875, . .	J. B. Graw, D. D.*	
1875, .	. Arthur W. Milby.*	
1876, . . .	Louis E. McComas.	
1877, . . .	M. C. Herman, ...	. . 1878
1877, . .	Joseph W. Hendrix, M. D.	
1877, . . .	S. L. Bowman, D. D.*	
1877, . .	William J. Sibley.	
1877, . . .	John M. Curtis, M. D.	
1877, . . .	Henry P. Hopkins.	
1877, . .	Thomas Mallalieu.	
1878, . . .	Wilbur F. Sadler.	
1878, . . .	Charles H. Mullin.	
1878, .	. Charles E. Hendrickson.	
1878, . . .	John T. Mitchell.	

OFFICERS OF THE BOARD OF TRUSTEES.

PRESIDENTS.

Elected. Ceased.

1783, John Dickinson, LL. D., ... 1808

1808, John King, D. D.,* 1808

1808, James Armstrong, ... 1824

1824, John Bannister Gibson, LL. D., ... 1829

1829, Andrew Carothers, ... 1833

1833, John Emory, D. D., Bishop of M. E. Church,* . 1834

1834, John Price Durbin, D. D.,* 1845

1842, Robert Emory, (*pro tem.*,)* 1844

1845, Robert Emory, D. D.,* 1847

1848, Beverly Waugh, D. D., (*pro tem.*,) Bishop of M.
E. Church,* 1848

1849, Jesse Truesdale Peck, D. D.,* 1852

1852, Charles Collins, D. D.,* 1860

1860, Herman Merrills Johnson, D. D., LL. D.,* . . 1868

1868, Robert L. Dashiell, D. D.,* 1872

1872, James A. McCauley, D. D.*

SECRETARIES.

1783, William Linn, D. D.,* 1784

1784, Thomas Duncan, LL. D., ... 1792

1792, Thomas Creigh, ... 1796

1796, James Duncan, ... 1806

1806, Alexander P. Lyon, ... 1808

1808, Andrew Carothers, ... 1814

1814, Isaac B. Parker, ... 1820

1820, James Hamilton, ... 1824

1824, Frederick Watts, ... 1828

Elected.	Ceased.
1828, Samuel A. McCoskry, D. D.,*	1831
1831, William M. Biddle,	1833
1833, Charles Bingham Penrose,	1837
1837, John McClintock, D. D., LL. D.,*	1848
1848, William Henry Allen, LL. D.,	1850
1850, James William Marshall,	1854
1854, Otis Henry Tiffany, D. D.,*	1857
1857, James William Marshall,	1858
1858, William Laws Boswell,*	1865
1865, John Keagy Stayman,	1868
1868, Charles Francis Himes, Ph. D.	

TREASURERS.

Elected.	Ceased.
1784, Samuel Laird,	1790
1790, Samuel Postlethwaite,	1798
1798, John Montgomery,	1808
1808, John Miller,	1821
1821, Andrew McDowell,	1833
1833, John J. Myers, M. D.,	1841
1841, William D. Seymour,	1854
1854, James William Marshall,	1861
1861, Samuel Dickinson Hillman,	1868
1868, John Keagy Stayman,	1868
1868, Charles Francis Himes, Ph. D.	

FACULTY OF DICKINSON COLLEGE.

PRESIDENTS.

Elected.   Ceased.

1784, Charles Nisbet, D. D.,* 1785

1785, Robert Davidson, D. D., (*pro tem.,*)* 1786

1786, Charles Nisbet, D. D.,* 1804

1804, Robert Davidson, D. D., (*pro tem.,*) 1809

1809. Jeremiah Atwater, D. D.,* 1815

1815, John McKnight, D. D., (*pro tem.,*)* 1816

1821, John Mitchell Mason, D. D.,* 1824

1824, William Neill, D. D.,* 1829

1830, Samuel B. How, D. D.,* 1832

1833, John Price Durbin, D. D.,* 1845

1842, Robert Emory, D. D., (*pro tem.,*)* 1844

1845, Robert Emory, D. D.,* 1848

1848, Jesse Truesdale Peck, D. D.,* 1852

1852, Charles Collins, D. D.,* 1860

1860, Herman Merrills Johnson, D. D.,* 1868

1868, Robert Lawrence Dashiell, D. D.,* 1872

1872, James Andrew McCauley, D. D.*

PROFESSORS AND LECTURERS.

1784, Charles Nisbet, D. D.,* Moral Philosophy, . . . 1804

1784, James Ross, A. M., Lat. and Gr. Lang. and Lit., 1792

1785, Robert Davidson, D. D., Hist., Geog., Chron.,
                       and Rhet., ... 1804

1804,   Moral Philosophy, . . 1809

1786, Robert Johnston, A. M., Math. and Nat. Phil., . . 1787

1792, James McCormick, A. M., Math. and Nat. Phil., 1814

Elected.		Ceased.
1795,	William Thomson, A. M., Lat. & Gr. Lang. & Lit.,	1804
1804,	John Borland, A. M., Lat. and Gr. Lang. and Lit.,	1805
1811,	Gr. Lang. and Lit., .	. 1812
1807,	John Hays, A. M.,* Lat. and Gr. Lang. and Lit.,	1809
1809,	Henry R. Wilson, A. M.,* Lat. & Gr. Lang. & Lit.,	1813
1809,	Jeremiah Atwater, D D.,* Moral Philosophy, . .	1815
1811,	Thomas Cooper, M. D., LL. D., Chem. & Nat. Phil.,	1815
1813.	Joseph Shaw, A. M.,* Lat. & Gr. Lang. & Lit., .	1815
1814,	Eugenius Nulty, A. M., Math., ...	1816
1814,	Claudius Berard, A. M., Mod. Lang., . .	. 1816
1815,	John McKnight, D. D.,* Moral Philosophy, . . .	1816
1816,	Gerard E. Stack, A. M., (*pro tem.*.) Lat. and Gr. Lang. and Lit., ...	1816
1821,	John M. Mason, D. D., Moral Philosophy, . . .	1824
1821,	Henry Vethake, LL. D., Math. and Nat. Phil.,	1829
1821,	—— Burns, Lat. and Gr. Lang. and Lit., . .	. 1822
1821,	Alexander McClelland, D. D.,* Rhet., Metaphys., and Eth., ...	1829
1822,	Joseph Spencer, A. M.,* Lat. & Gr. Lang. & Lit.,	1830
1825,	Louis Mayer, D. D.,* Mod. Lang., ...	. 1826
1826,	John W. Vethake, A. M., M. D., Lect. on Chem.,	1827
1827,	John K. Finley, M. D., Lecturer on Chem.,	. 1828
1828,	Prof. Chem. & Nat. Phil.,	1829
1830,	Charles Dexter Cleveland, A. M., Lat, and Gr. Lang. and Lit., ...	1832
1830,	Alexander McFarlane, A. M.,* Math., ...	1832
1830,	Henry D. Rogers, A. M., Nat. Sci., . . .	1831
1831,	Lemuel G. Olmstead, A. M.,* Lecturer on Chem.,	1832
1834,	Merritt Caldwell, A. M., Math., ...	1836
1836,	Metaphys. & Polit. Econ.,	1848
1834,	Robert Emory, A. M., Lat. & Gr. Lang. & Lit., .	1840
1845,	Moral Philosophy, . .	1848

Elected.   Ceased.

1834, John Reed, LL. D., Laws, ... 1850

1835, John M. Keagy, M. D., Nat. Sci., ... 1836

1836, William Henry Allen, A. M., Lect. on Nat. Sci., 1837

1837,   Prof. Nat. Sci., . . 1848

1848,   Philos. & Eng. Lit., 1850

1836, John McClintock, A. M., Math., ... 1840

1840,   Lat. & Gr. Lang. & Lit., 1848

1837, Stephan Asbury Roszel, A. M., Lat. and Gr. Lang.
and Lit., ... 1838

1840, Thomas Emory Sudler, A. M., Math., ... 1851

1845, Spencer F. Baird, A. M., Nat. Hist.,   . . 1848

1848,   Nat. Sci., . .   1850

1846, Charles E. Blumenthal, A. M., Mod. Lang. & Heb.,1854

1846, George R. Crooks, A. M.,* (Adjunct,) Lat. and
Gr. Lang. and Lit., ... 1848

1848, Otis Henry Tiffany, A. M.,* (Adjunct,) Math., . 1851

1851,   Math., . 1857

1848, James W. Marshall, A. B., (Adjunct,) Lat. and
Gr. Lang. and Lit., . 1850

1850,   Lat. and Gr. Lang.
and Lit., .   . . 1860

1860,   Lat. and Fr. Lang., 1862

1850, Erastus Wentworth, D. D.,* Nat. Sci., ... 1854

1850, Herman M. Johnson, A. M., D. D.,* Philos. and
Eng. Lit.,1860

1860,   Moral Phil.,1868

1852, Charles Collins, D. D.,* Moral Philosophy, . . . 1860

1854, William Carlisle Wilson, A. M., Lect. on Nat. Sci.,1855

1855,   Prof. Nat. Sci.,   . . . 1865

1854, Alexander J. Schem, A. M., Mod. Lang. and Heb.,1860

1857, William Laws Boswell, A. M.,* Math., ... 1860

1860,   Gr. & Ger. Lang., 1865

Elected.   Ceased.

1860, Samuel Dickinson Hillman, A. M., Math., . . . 1874
1861, John Keagy Stayman, A. M., (Adjunct,) Lat. and
                                    Fr. Lang., . . . 1862
1862,   Prof. Lat. and Fr. Lang., 1867
1867,   Prof. Lat. and Gr. Lang.
                                  and Lit., . . 1869
1869,   Prof. Phil. and Eng. Lit., 1874
1862, James Hutchison Graham, LL. D., Laws.
1865, Charles Francis Himes, Ph. D., Nat. Sci.
1866, S. L. Bowman, A. M.,* Gr. & Heb. Lang. & Lit., 1867
1868,   Bib. Lang. and Lit., . . 1871
1868, Robert L. Dashiell, D. D.,* Moral Philosophy, . 1872
1868, William Trickett, A. B.,* (Adjunct,) Phil. & Eng.
                               Lit., ... 1869
1869,   A. M., (Adjunct,) Mod. Lang., 1870
1872, 70.   Mod. Lang., ... 1874
1869, Henry M. Harman, D. D.,* Ancient Lang. & Lit.
1872, James Andrew McCauley, D. D.,* Moral Philos.
1874. Joshua A. Lippincott, A. M.,* Math.
1874, William R. Fisher, Mod. Lang., ...   1876
1874, Charles J. Little, A. M., Phil. and Eng. Lit.

TUTORS.

1785, Robert Johnston, A. M., Math., ... 1786
1788, James McCormick, A. B., Math., ... 1792
1792, Charles Houston, A. B., ... 1793
1793, Henry L. Davis, A. B., ... 1794
1805, John Hayes, A. B., ... 1807
1810, Frederick Aigster, M. D., Nat. Phil. and Chem., . 1811
1810, John McClure, A. B., ... 1811
1812, Robert C. Grier, A. B., ... 1813
1838, Thomas Verner Moore, A. B., ... 1839

Elected.   Ceased.

1839, John Zug, A. B.,   .   .   1840

1839, William Smith Waters, A. B.,   1840

1851, Amos Farry Musselman. A. B.,   1854

1854, Benjamin Arbogast, A. B.,   . 1856

www.ingramcontent.com/pod-product-compliance
Lightning Source LLC
Chambersburg PA
CBHW020014030726
47500CB00002B/577